STAR WARS
FORCES OF DESTINY™

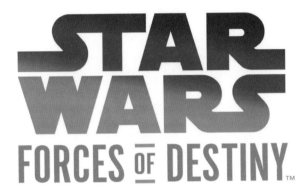

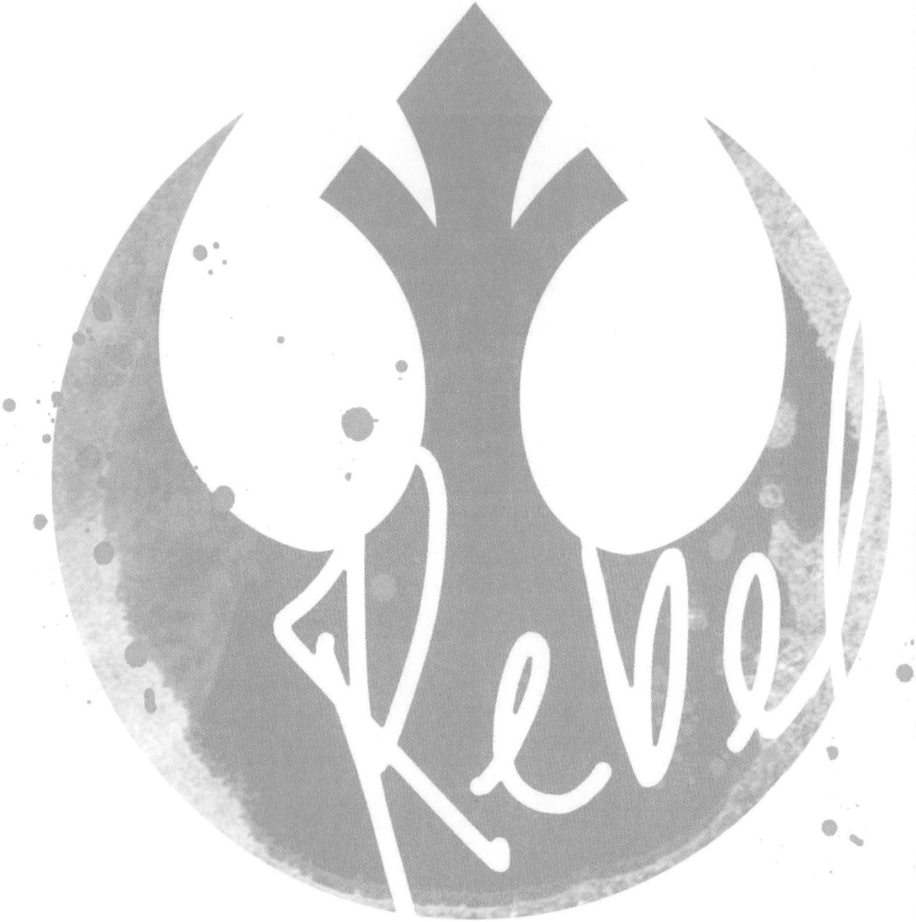
Rebel

STAR WARS

FORCES OF DESTINY™

The Rey Chronicles

Written by
Emma Carlson Berne

DISNEY
LUCASFILM
PRESS
Los Angeles • New York

ABDO
Spotlight

ABDOBOOKS.COM

Reinforced library bound edition published in 2020 by Spotlight, a division of ABDO
PO Box 398166, Minneapolis, Minnesota 55439. Spotlight produces high-quality
reinforced library bound editions for schools and libraries.
Published by agreement with Disney • Lucasfilm Press.

Printed in the United States of America, North Mankato, Minnesota.
042019
092019

THIS BOOK CONTAINS
RECYCLED MATERIALS

P R E S S

Library of Congress Control Number: 2018966042

Publisher's Cataloging-in-Publication Data

Names: Carlson Berne, Emma, author. | Disney–Lucasfilm Press, illustrator.
Title: The Rey chronicles / by Emma Carlson Berne; illustrated by Disney–Lucasfilm
    Press.
Description: Minneapolis, Minnesota : Spotlight, 2020. | Series: Star Wars: forces of
    destiny chapter books
Summary: Follow Rey as she uncovers a threat to the Millennium Falcon, helps a
    hapless happabore, and crosses paths with Teedo.
Identifiers: ISBN 9781532143281 (lib. bdg.)
Subjects: LCSH: Star wars, forces of destiny (Television program)--Juvenile fiction. |
    Rey (Fictitious character)--Juvenile fiction. | Rescue work--Juvenile fiction. |
    Adventure stories--Juvenile fiction. | Space--Juvenile fiction. | Comic books,
    strips, etc--Juvenile fiction.
Classification: DDC [FIC]--dc23

Spotlight
A Division of ABDO
abdobooks.com

CONTENTS

A MESSAGE FROM MAZ

Hello, friend. I am glad you've found my campfire. Sit down. There is tea in the kettle. Ah—I see you are tired. Here is a blanket for your shoulders. See what I have found in one of my trunks? That's right—ikopi antlers. Shed years ago. I found them in the forest. See how strong the bone is? Sharp at the ends. Unyielding. Take it. There you go. Hold it in your hands. The bone is smooth and heavy—lovely to look at. Often people don't realize

how strong the antlers are until the stags fight.
Then they see what powerful weapons they are.

You too, friend. I see you looking at the
kettle. The tea is almost ready. You are ready
for a rest, though you are tough, I can tell.
Tough like a bone. Remember that sometimes
being tough means helping others—and then
often they will help you in return.

Here, the tea is ready. I will pour you a cup.
Feel the steam on your face. Rest, my friend.

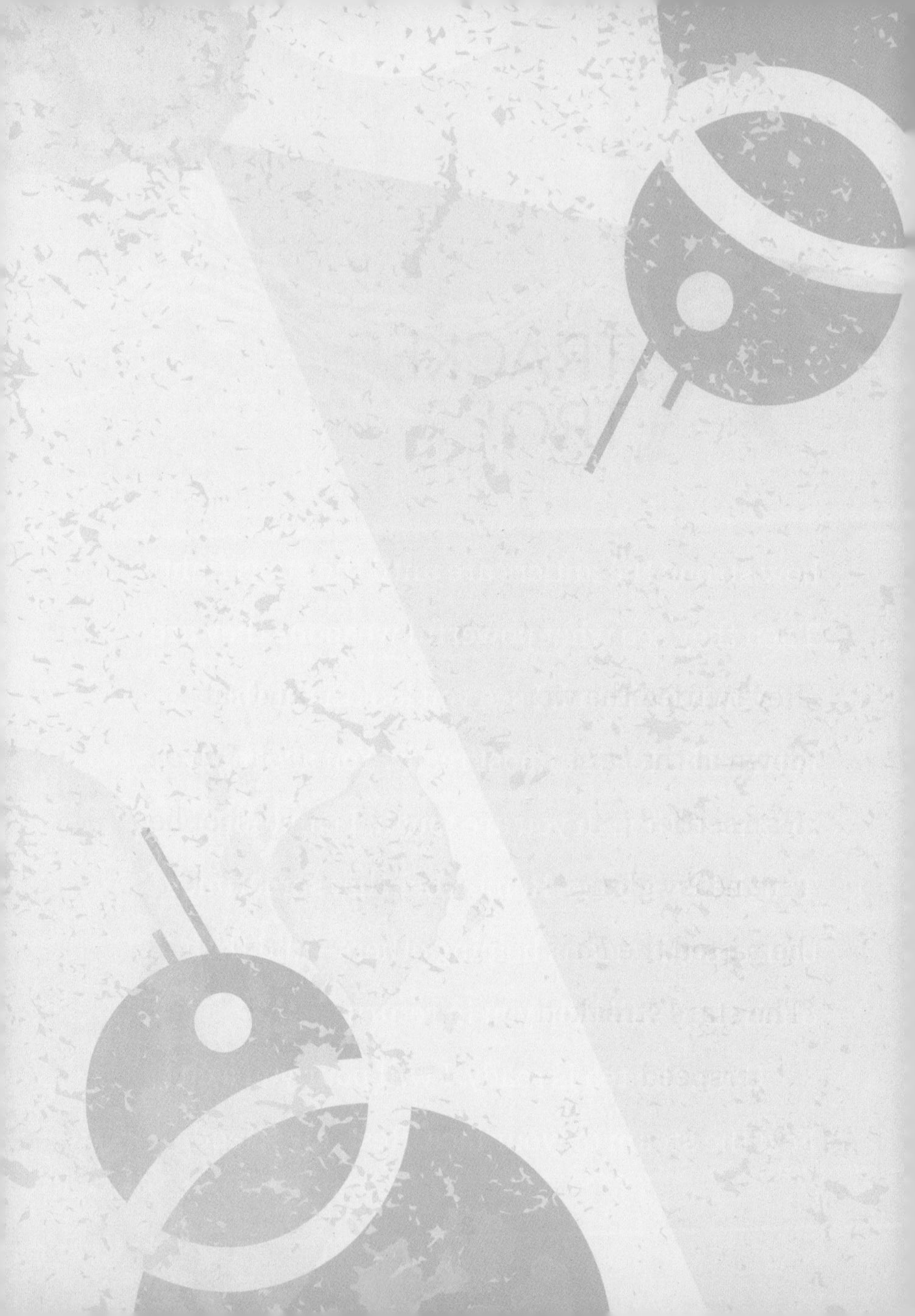

TRACKER TROUBLE

Rey twirled the worn copilot's seat and sat down at the controls of the *Millennium Falcon*. Han settled into the captain's seat and shot her an uneasy glance. Rey looked over at him as he patted the *Falcon*'s scarred control panel. The stars streaked by outside, blurred by the hyperspeed.

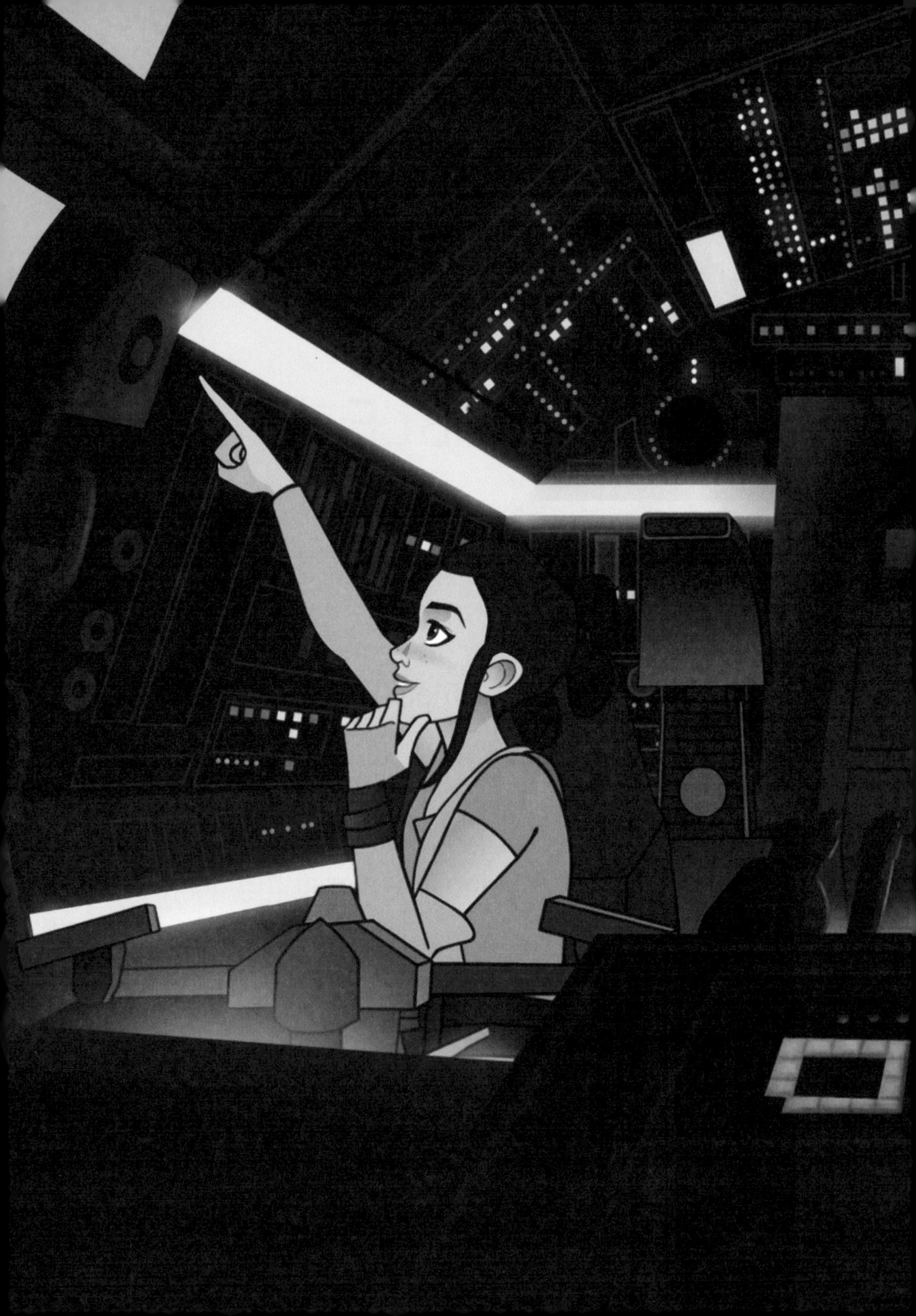

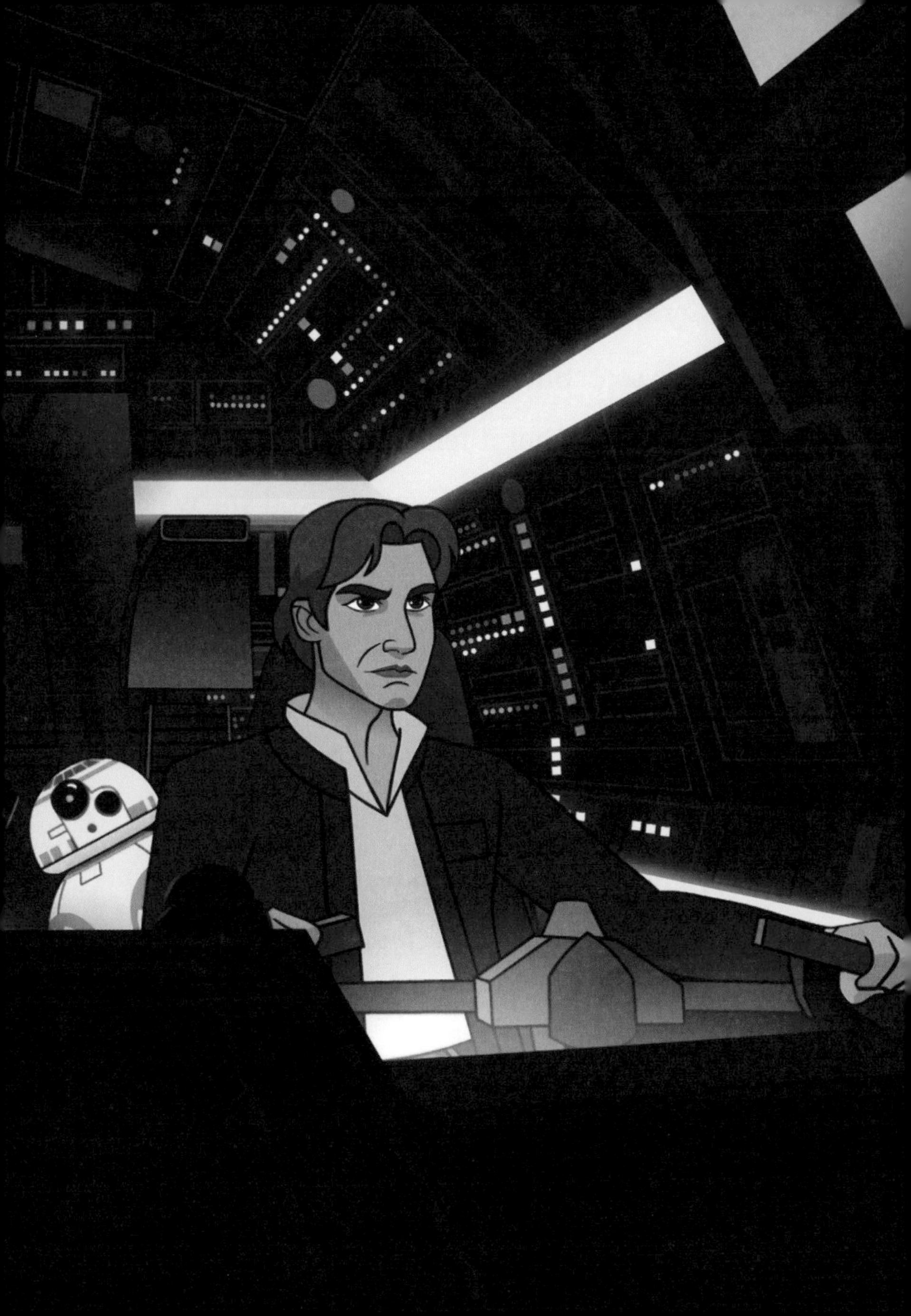

"Okay." Han flicked a few switches. "Now. Once we get to Maz's castle, keep your head down and leave it to me."

Rey smiled and patted the arm of the copilot's seat. She looked around the cockpit. This must be what it felt like to be part of a crew, like she'd always wanted. And she was off Jakku, away from the sand and the heat and the need for constant vigilance—and Unkar. Rey felt something loosen inside her— something that had been knotted so tight all those years, she had hardly felt it anymore.

All her life, she'd been waiting to leave Jakku. Now she *had* left Jakku, and she'd flown for real for the first time, and she'd fought the First Order for the first time. As she thought back on the day, Rey felt dizzy with her life's sudden acceleration.

The First Order had called in the air strike soon after Rey met Finn at Niima Outpost on Jakku. The two TIE fighters had zoomed down on them firing, hitting the sand and spraying it everywhere. She, Finn, and BB-8 sprinted toward a quadjumper as the TIEs' laser blasts screamed into the ground behind them. Then a blast hit the quadjumper, which exploded into a ball of flames.

She shouted at Finn and BB-8 to run for a wreck nearby. She was familiar with the ship, but for as long as she could remember, it had sat motionless on the sand, baking in the white-hot sun. The sweat poured down her face and neck as she flipped switches from the pilot's seat, firing up the engines, while Finn got ready to operate the gun from below. The ship roared to life, bumping and dragging along the sand, then soared with heart-lifting force into the blue sky.

They shot through the ruins of rusted space hulks that lay in the desert, Rey hanging on to the controls as the *Falcon* shuddered and creaked. In the gun turret, Finn tried to return fire as BB-8 rolled around behind Rey like a loose grav-ball until he stabilized himself with magnetic cables. Then they were hit, heading straight for a collision with a massive piece of junk. Gritting her teeth, Rey grabbed the thruster and fired it, twisting the yoke at the same time to turn them sharply and soar straight toward the heavens. She was flying, after all those years of practicing on dead ships—and nothing had ever felt more natural.

Finn managed to take out one of the TIEs, but then the *Falcon*'s gun sustained a hit. Finn couldn't aim the gun anymore. He shouted at Rey that they'd have to shake off the other TIE. It was time for some desperate flying. Up ahead were the dead, hollowed-out thrust rings of a giant Super Star Destroyer. Her heart pounding in her ears, hands wet with sweat, Rey flew the *Falcon* directly into one of the thrusters like a fly into the mouth of a happabore.

The TIE was right on her tail, dodging and weaving through the innards of the ship. Then Rey saw it—a blocked passageway at the end. The TIE locked on to them. She could feel it.

Flying on nothing but nerve, she jerked the yoke to the right, sending the *Falcon* through a gap in the wreck's hull and soaring out into the blue sky again.

Then she pushed the *Falcon* down. They had to lose height fast; she had to line up the shot for Finn. They were flipping in the sky and the TIE was on them, and then Finn fired right as the ship's gun turret rotated toward the TIE. He made the shot, and the TIE exploded just as Rey strained for the stabilizer, reached it, and deployed it.

The *Falcon* righted itself, smoothed out— and that was it. They'd won. With her heart leaping in her chest, Rey aimed them out of the Jakku atmosphere and into space. *I'm leaving Jakku!* her mind was screaming. *Leaving!*

She
and Finn
had one
moment of
joy, shouting

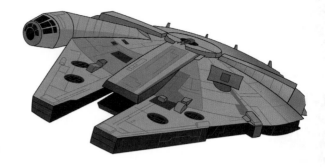

at each other with all the excitement of having

defeated First Order fighters in a creaky

piece of space junk, when the motivator blew,

filling the propulsion tank and giving them

only minutes before the tank overflowed,

contaminating the air supply.

She had just applied the patch when the

whole ship went dark. They were being sucked

into what they thought was a First Order ship.

The *Falcon* was disabled; the bigger ship was

overriding all their controls. No amount of

flying would get them out of that predicament.

Scrambling to think of a solution, sure that stormtroopers would be there any moment, they hid in a cargo hatch. Then the door slid open, and instead of stormtroopers, Han and Chewie appeared.

Han was about to agree to help them get BB-8 to the Resistance base when they heard a dull thudding somewhere in the depths of the ship. Han took off running, and Rey and Finn followed.

Han was hauling rathtars, it turned out— huge, slimy, tentacled creatures with circular mouths and thousands of teeth. Before Rey could fully absorb what was happening, members of the Guavian Death Gang boarded the ship, followed in short order by the gang known as Kanjiklub. Han stuffed Rey and Finn into a compartment with orders not to move until he'd gotten rid of the intruders. But from what Rey and Finn overheard from their hiding place, Han was trapped between the two gangs. They both wanted money from him—and there didn't seem to be any good way out.

Rey and Finn crawled through the bowels of the freighter until Rey saw a fuse panel and a light flicked on in her head. If she could just reset the fuses—they could close the corridor doors remotely and both gangs would be trapped. It was a brilliant plan—except that she reset the wrong fuses. Instead of closing the corridor doors, she *opened* the doors of the rathtars' holding cells.

Rathtars rolled down the corridors, tentacles waving, giant mouths gaping. The gangs, thrown into confusion, fired and scattered. Rey and Finn managed to find a hatch back into the main corridor of the freighter, only to come face to teeth with a rathtar. Rey just had time to see the giant waving ball roaring at them hungrily before she and Finn took off in the opposite direction.

Heart pounding in her ears, adrenaline pumping through her veins, Rey ran as hard as she'd ever run. Suddenly, Finn screamed. The rathtar had snared him, its tentacle like a chain around his waist. It was dragging him backward along the metal floor. She screamed for him, but the rathtar had him in its tentacles, holding him high in the air. It rolled backward with surprising speed, dragging him around a corner and down a distant corridor, leaving Rey with nothing but the sound of his panicked screams.

Rey ran through the ship, yelling for Finn, frantic to do something, anything. She rushed up to a bank of monitors only to see images of Finn being dragged down a corridor. *Do something!* She could see the rathtar yanking Finn through a doorway. He screamed again. Rey stared at the screen. She felt her mind grow calm. She focused on the screen and pressed the button to activate the door, slamming it shut with the rathtar on one side and Finn on the other. Finn hit the floor as the door severed the rathtar's tentacles, which flopped and slithered next to him.

Rey ran down the corridor, relief flooding her. Finn wasn't dead—but they still had to escape the ship. Panting and covered in rathtar slime, they ran together through the freighter and out into the main hangar where Han and Chewie were standing at the base of the *Falcon*. Chewie was hurt! Han shouted directions at them as they scrambled onto the ship. Rey slid into the copilot's seat, and she and Han powered up the *Falcon* as Chewie howled in pain in the medbay.

Suddenly, a huge mouth and tentacles were plastered to the windshield and Rey shrieked. One of the rathtars had found them and attached itself to the front of the ship. Meanwhile, the surviving gang members started firing from the ground.

Han applied thrust, but the ship stalled halfway through its lift.

"Compressor," Rey ventured, and pointed at the control panel. Han shot her a glance. She hit the switch. The ship rose, engines firing. Han jumped to lightspeed and they braced themselves as the *Falcon* launched forward, pulverizing the rathtar and blasting through the wall of the freighter, then shooting them out into the vast darkness of space beyond.

Now everyone was safe, and they were on their way to Takodana to see Han's friend Maz Kanata, in the hopes that she could help them get to the Resistance. The information BB-8 was carrying about Luke Skywalker was too important to let fall into the wrong hands.

Rey stretched her arms over her head and exhaled.

"All in all, things have gone pretty well, don't you think—"

Her words were cut off as the *Falcon* gave a sudden, massive jolt.

"What the—" Han thumbed the controls.

"We dropped out of hyperspace," he said. "What's going on?"

Rey's stomach plunged.

"Did you do a full sweep for tracking devices?" she asked Han.

"This isn't sounding good!" Finn yelled somewhere behind them.

"Chewie!" Han called over his shoulder. "You scanned it, right?"

Chewie roared in assent.

Han looked over at Rey. "So we should be okay. Probably just a malfunction of some kind."

"Ahhh . . ." Rey shook her head.

"Unkar's been using a new kind of modified tracking device. We might need to do a visual check." Thoughts were whirring through her mind.

"I'll get the hyperdrive back online," Han said. "You go check the rest of the ship with Chewie." He twisted around and eyed BB-8. "You, Ball, scan the ship again."

The droid beeped in response as Rey ran down the corridor to Chewbacca and Finn.

"What's going on?" Finn asked.

"Unkar hired me to help him fix ships," Rey told him. "I never put a tracker on the *Falcon*, but he may have." She stopped and glanced at Chewie.

"The problem is," she continued, "I don't know exactly where Unkar would have planted it. It could be anywhere."

Rey pulled open an access panel and scanned the mass of wires inside. Nothing. She slammed the door shut. They had to hurry. Finn trailed behind them, looking around even though he obviously had no idea what he was looking for. Sweat rolled down Rey's face, pooling at the base of her neck.

Chewie roared a suggestion and her head jerked up.

"Chewie, that's it!" She resisted the urge to hug the Wookiee. "That is brilliant! You are good. Come on." She walked as fast as she could toward the back of the ship, Chewie by her side.

"Hey, did you guys figure out where it is?" Finn asked, struggling to keep up with them.

Chewie roared.

"What did he say?" Finn looked confusedly at Rey.

Rey grabbed Finn by the arm.

"He thinks we should look near the active sensor pulse generator. Unkar could've hid it there undetected"—she took a breath—"since the augmenter would boost the modulation." She stopped and looked at Finn.

He raised his eyebrows.

"Sorry I asked," he said.

Rey grinned.

"Ships are kind of my thing."

Finn nodded slowly.

"Yeah. I got that."

The active sensor pulse generator flashed red at the back of the ship. They skidded to a stop in front of it. Chewie opened the panel. Cradled in a nest of wires, a small circular black object flashed red. Rey slapped Chewie's shoulder.

"There it is!" she cried.

"Hang on, I got this," Finn said, pushing her aside.

"No, wait!" Rey shouted, realizing what Finn was about to do. Chewie barked a warning, as well.

It was too late. Finn pulled out the tracker,

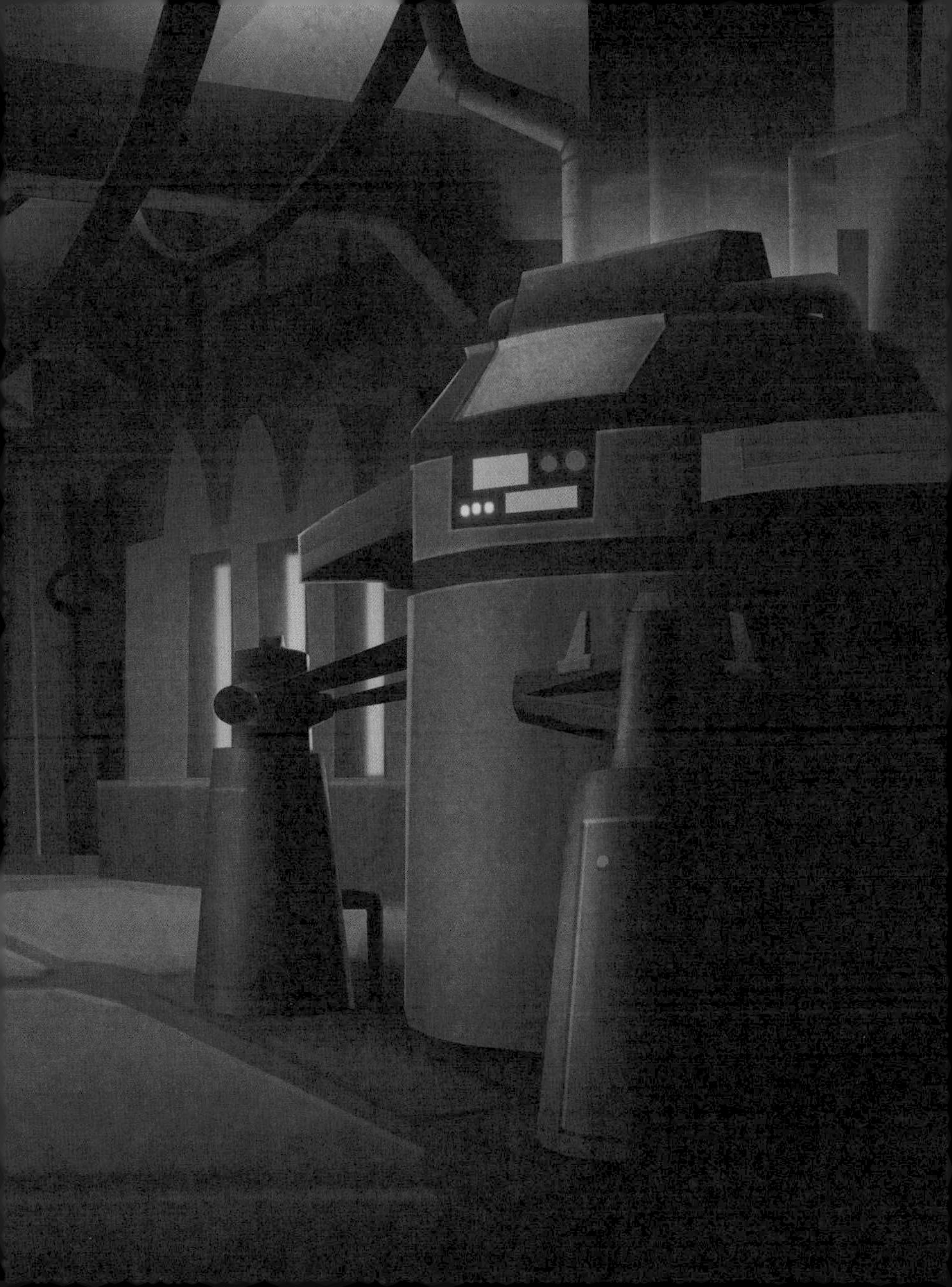

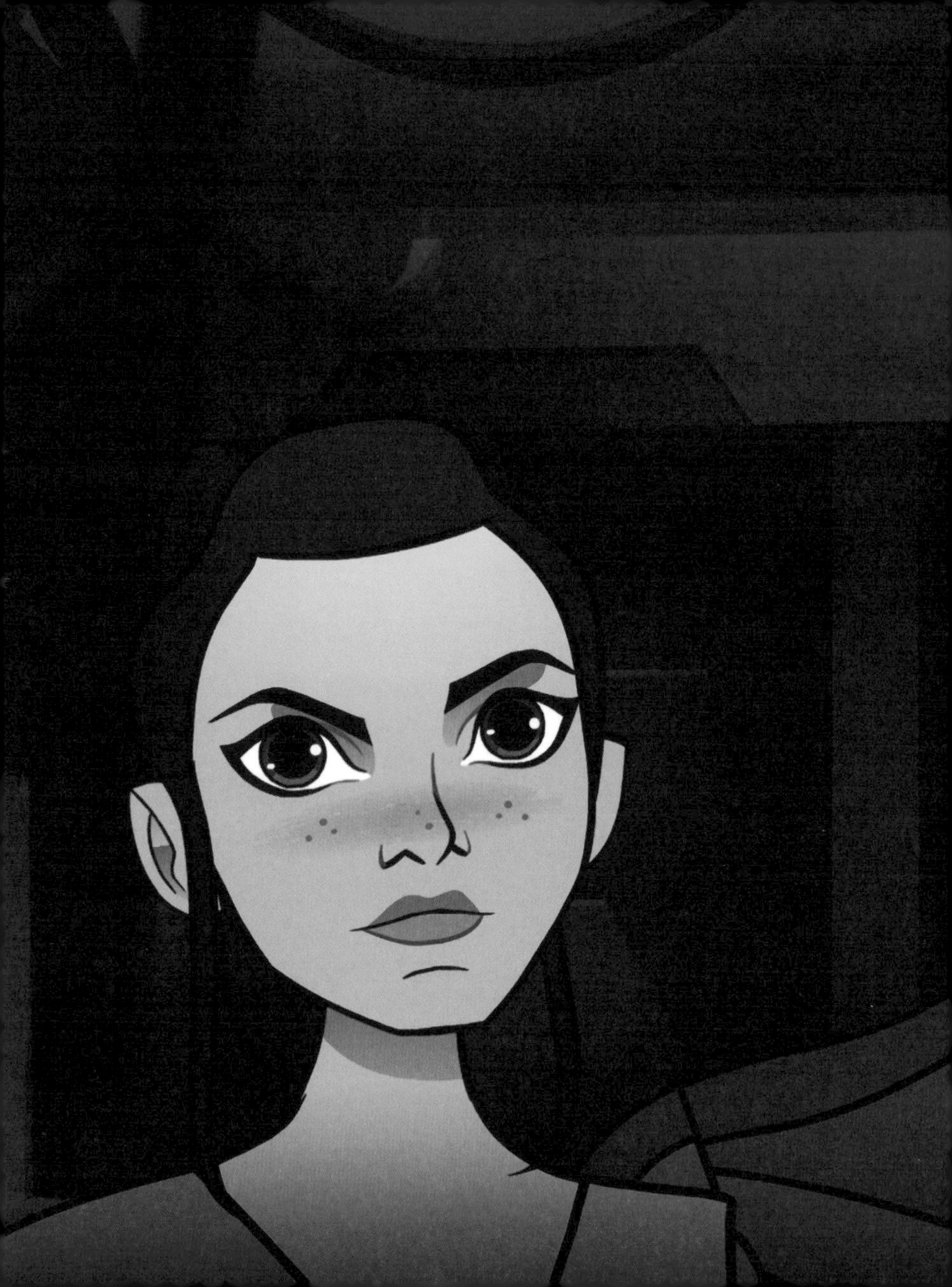

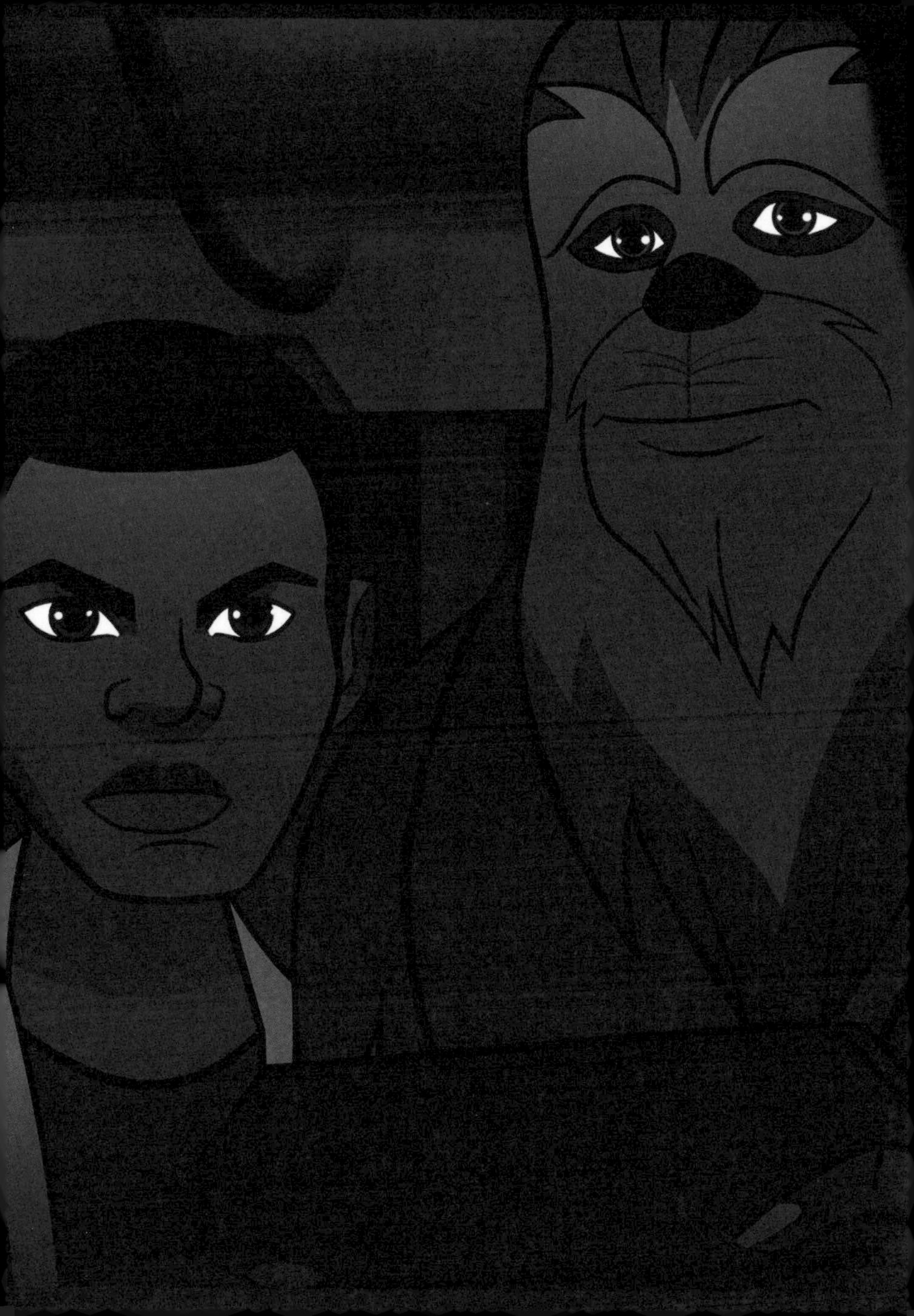

looking proud of himself. Immediately, the ship gave a tremendous shake, throwing them all off balance.

"What? What did I do?" Finn yelled, holding the device up in one hand.

"It's rigged!" Rey shouted over the shaking of the ship. She grabbed a panel handle behind her and braced her feet. Chewie roared and pointed. The device was beeping. Finn stood frozen.

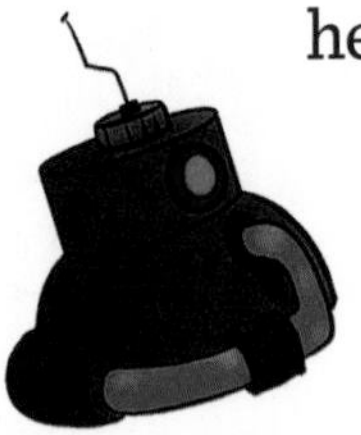

Chewie grabbed the tracker from Finn as the ship gave another massive shake, the floor dropping beneath their feet.

"Chewie! Get the tracker to the airlock! It's going to explode!" Rey yelled. Chewie roared. Rey fell against Finn, who was still standing with his mouth open.

"Go warn Han!" she shouted at him. He stared at her for an instant, his eyes wide, then ran.

In the cockpit, Han hunched intently over the control panel.

"Hyperdrive's back on!" he announced, punching a button. BB-8 chirped. The cockpit door banged open so hard it ricocheted back in Finn's face.

"Solo, we've found a bomb!" he yelled at Han.

"A bomb?" Han asked.

"Yes! Just get ready to punch it!" Finn said.

Back in the hold, Rey and Chewie stumbled over to the airlock. Chewie roared, holding the device.

"Now!" Rey said.

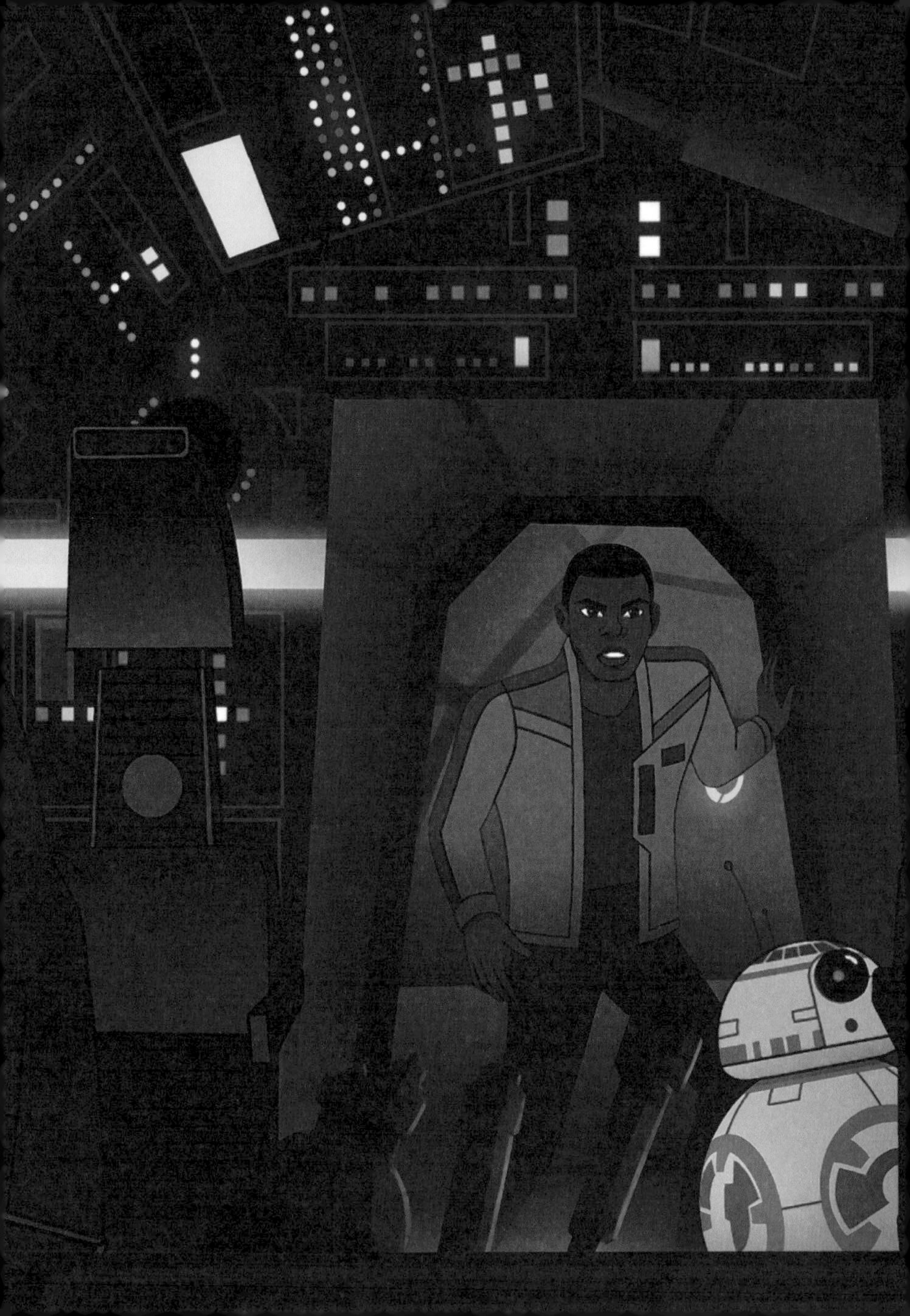

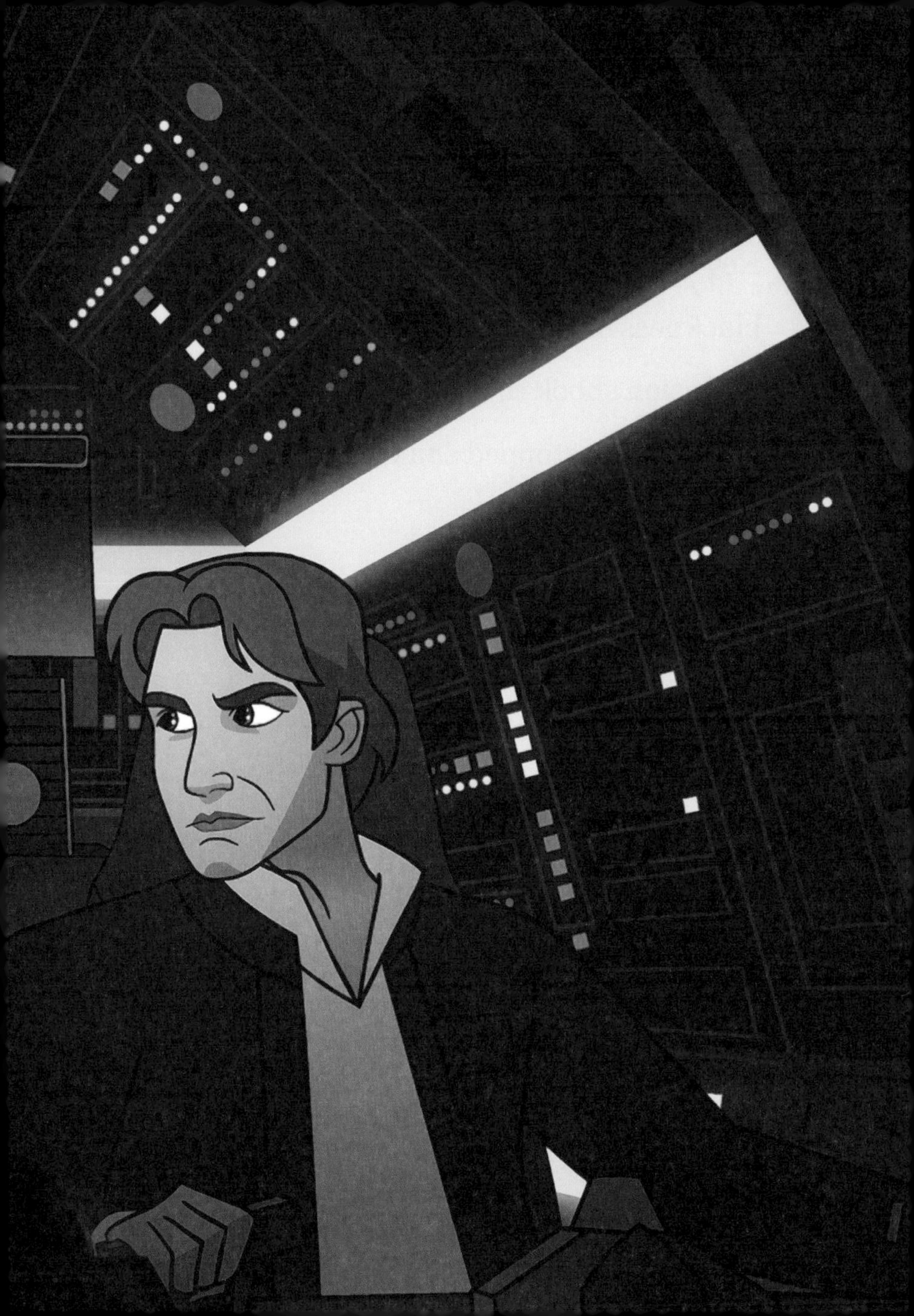

Chewie threw the airlock handle and tossed the tracker in. Through the window, Rey saw a blossom of fire explode in the blackness of space as if in slow motion. The explosion shook the ship.

The ship stopped shaking. Beautiful silence descended.

A short while later, they all lay sprawled in the ship's main hold. Rey couldn't stop smiling. Chewie couldn't, either.

Han looked from one to the other, one eyebrow raised.

"Great catch, kid," he said to Rey.

Finn nudged her in the ribs. Rey tried to look serious, but she couldn't keep the sloppy grin off her face.

"Thanks," she said. "We make a pretty good team." Then she followed Han into the cockpit. They were back on their way to Takodana.

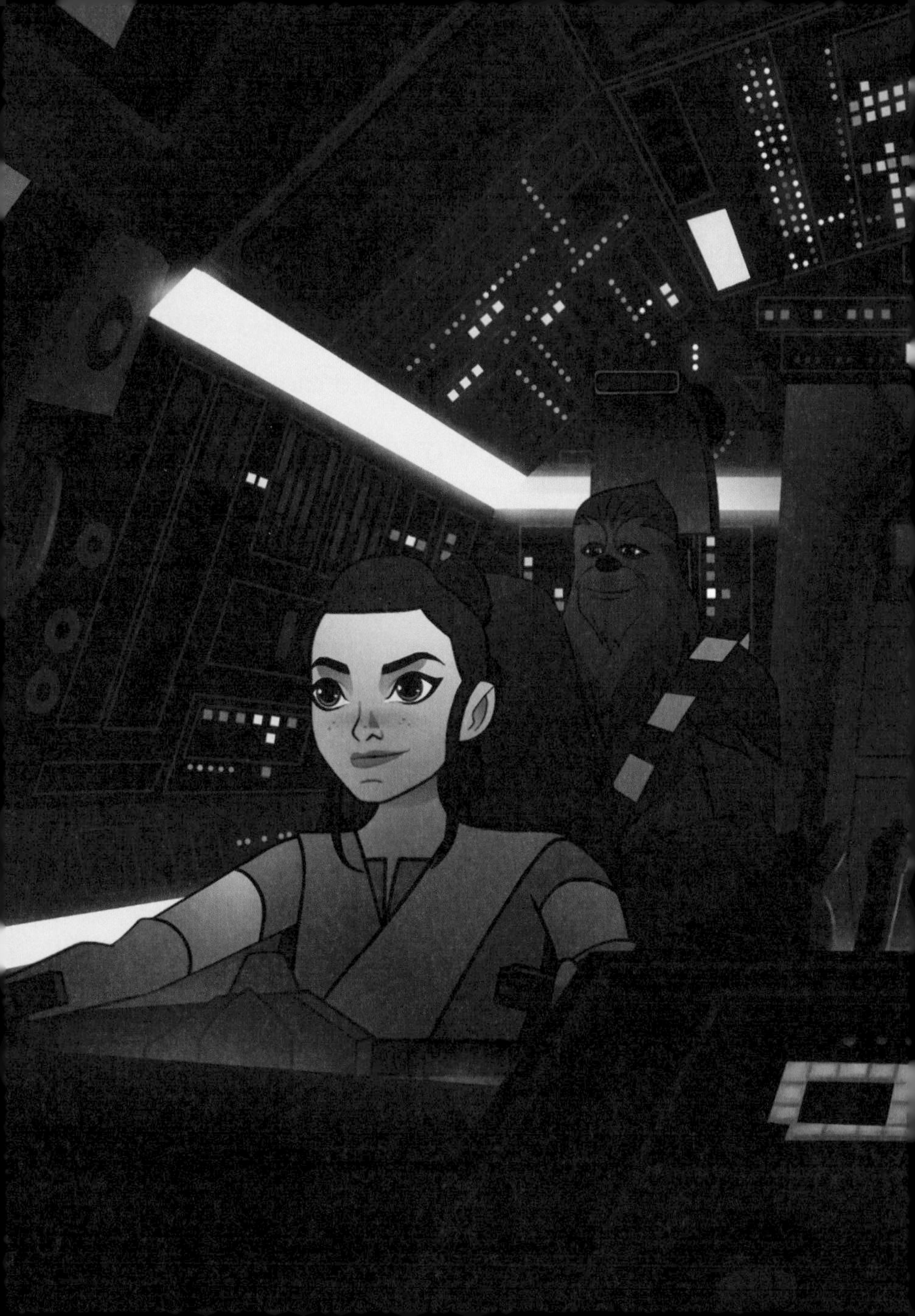

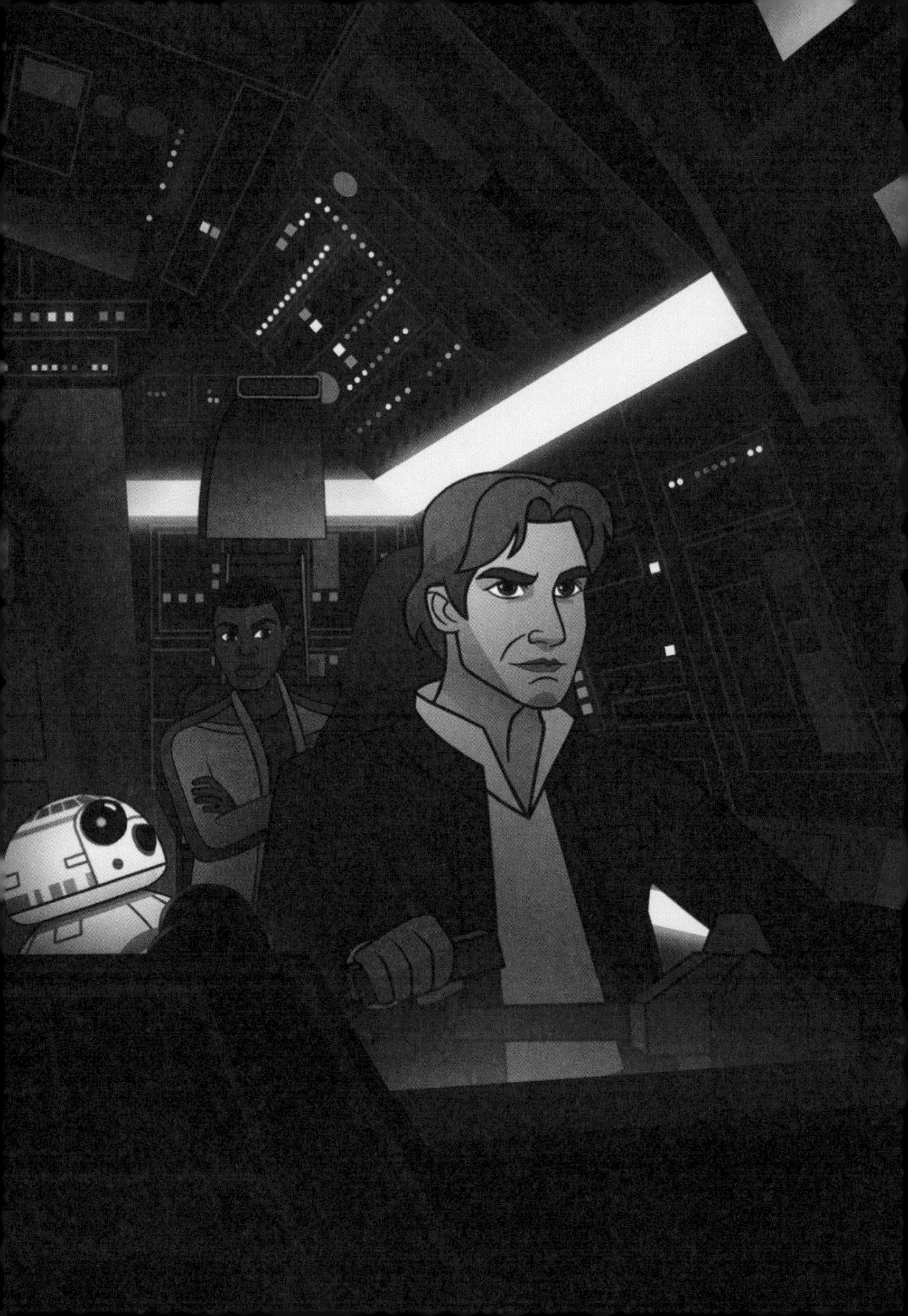

REY AND THE HAPPABORE

Rey bent low over the handles of her speeder, zipping across the familiar hot yellow sands of Jakku. The scorching wind blew the sweat from her face as fast as it could form. Her stomach rumbled. It had been a lean week. She'd been scavenging everywhere but finding nothing good—only a magnetic coupling, and

Unkar had given her only a quarter portion for it.

The Pilgrim's Road stretched before her. It was barely a road—mostly a path worn by happabores over the years as they trudged to the drinking troughs at Niima Outpost or Old Meru's. The Sitter came into view as a tiny dot far to her right, away from the road, almost to Carbon Ridge. The dot grew larger and turned into a tower with an old man perched on top. He was there sunrise to sunset—a wispy, sunbleached bit of humanity. Some thought he was a prophet, but Rey doubted that. If he was, wouldn't he find something better to do than sit in the blazing sun all day? She could see a line of three Teedos trudging up the stairs carved into the outside of the tower. They kept the Sitter alive—taking him thwip flesh and water.

Rey zipped past the Sitter, making him a gray-and-white blur, then left him behind. Carbon Ridge loomed next, low and ominous in the sun. Rey knew better than to scavenge there; rockslides cascaded down the mountains at any time of the day or night. Those who prowled around there might dislodge a little stone—and find themselves at the bottom of a canyon with fifty metric tons of rock on top of them. One learned such things pretty fast on Jakku.

Niima Outpost came into view, with its sprawling stalls, hunks of machinery lying around, traders arguing, scavengers dragging up loads on their sledges, and Unkar's booth at the center of it all. Unkar sat there like a squat jellyfish watching over his kingdom. *Blobfish,* Rey liked to call him in her mind. He liked her for her skills, though; she could fix anything and was great at scavenging Jakku's ship graveyard for parts. It was important to be useful on a world like Jakku.

Rey killed the motor and dismounted. Lerux Talley's intelligence better have been good. Another hungry night and she wasn't sure she'd have the energy to scavenge the next day. Unkar eyed her from behind the counter of his concession stand. It was actually an old cargo crawler, but he'd rigged it with monitors so his security thugs could make sure no one got too close.

The scanty cloth awning overhead did little to ward off the white sun. A little fan whirled behind Unkar's shoulder. The washing tables were crowded, filled with sunbaked scavengers scrubbing the sand from their salvage. She'd spent many hours at those tables, working the sand out of the crevices of fuel pumps and boosters, listening to the other scavengers gossip. It was a good place to pick up bits of intelligence. Sometimes the newer scavengers let slip where they'd found some valuable wrecks. She knew never to do that, though, always keeping the location of a wreck to herself until she'd stripped it *and* been paid by

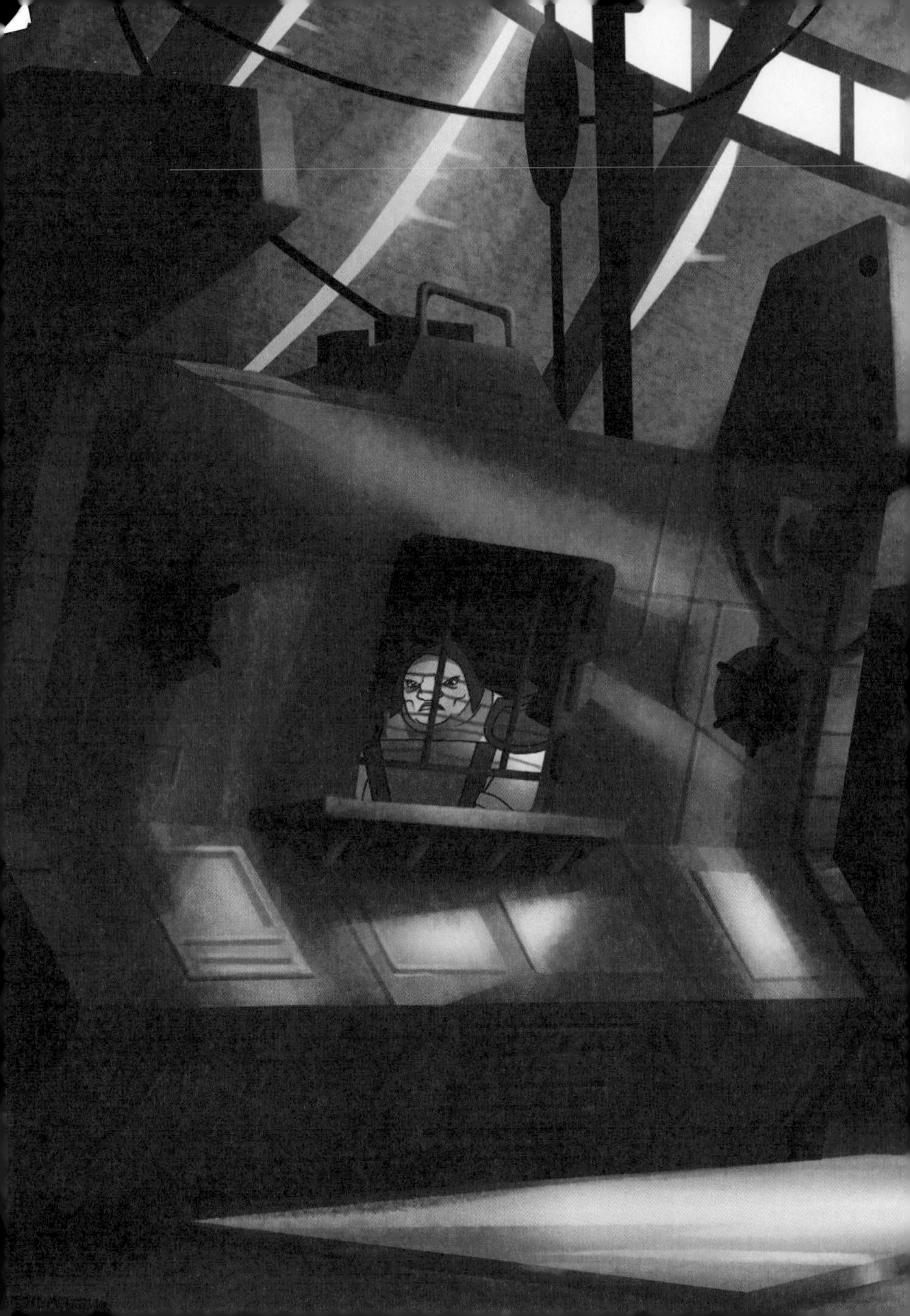

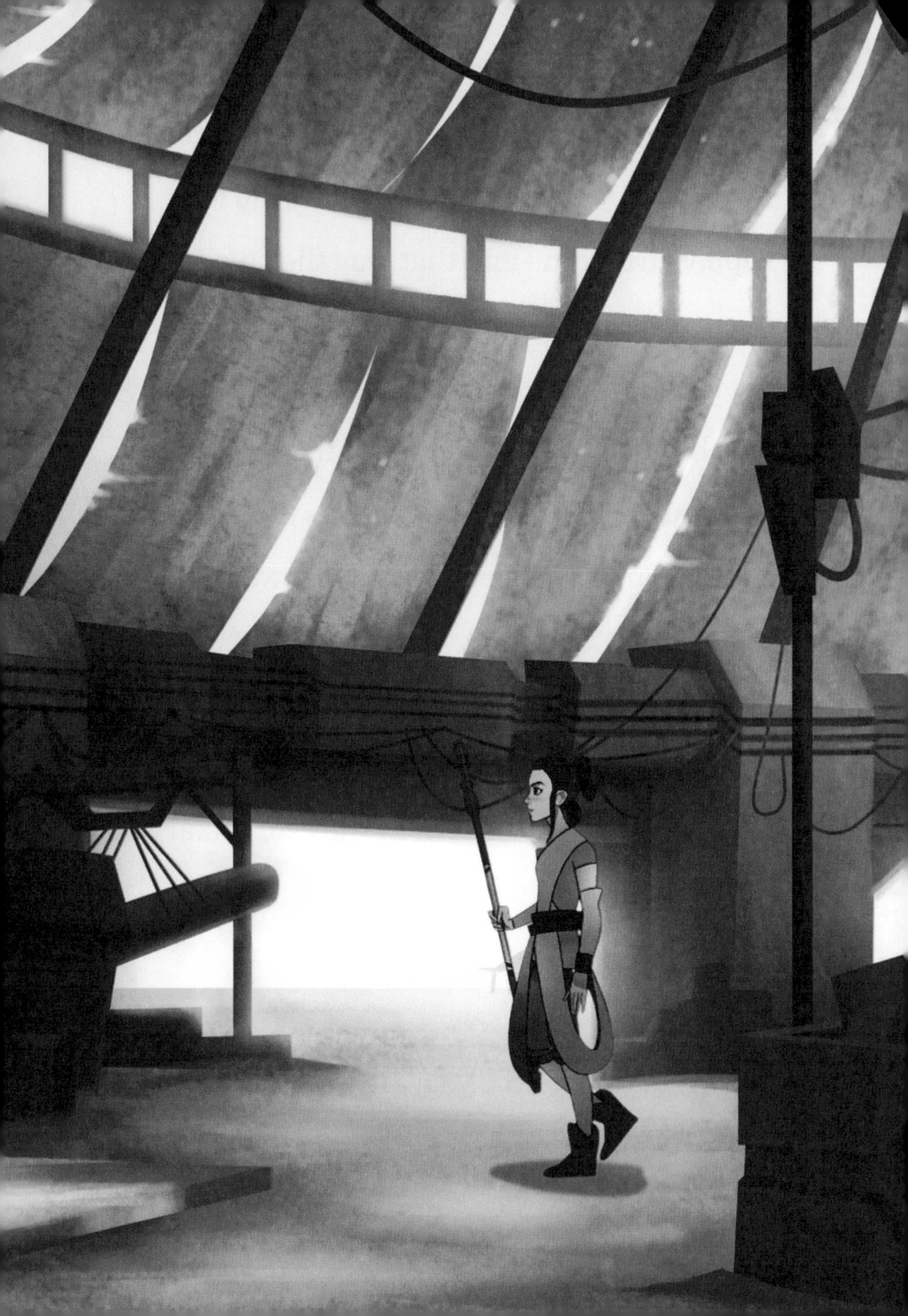

Unkar. And much as she didn't like it—she had to be paid by Unkar. He controlled the food supply on Jakku—and that was the only form of currency. Back in the early days, Unkar and his thugs had taken tons of rations out of the old ships. Now they kept the rations guarded and traded them for scrap. It was the only food source—and Rey needed food. She was always hungry.

"I hear you're paying ten portions to anyone able to a haul a scrap heap back to Niima Outpost." She looked him in the eye. Unkar could smell weakness like a sandsnake could smell a rat.

He snorted.

"That's no job for you, girl." He flapped

his hand at her and turned away to stuff a tuanulberry in his mouth.

Rey stiffened. The blood pounded in her forehead.

"And why not?" she demanded.

A smile stretched his flabby mouth.

"You can't do it by yourself, and you have no friends, scavenger." A fleck of tuanulberry flew from his lips and landed on Rey's shoulder. She brushed it off.

"Give me the coordinates and I'll prove you wrong," she snapped.

Unkar paused and eyed her. Just to Rey's left, a Teedo was pounding a sheet of metal with repetitive tings. He stopped, hammer in midair, listening to their conversation.

Unkar's smile broadened, showing his yellow teeth.

"All right. I'll give you the coordinates." He leaned forward.

"But if you don't bring anything back . . . I get your speeder."

Her speeder! The speeder she'd built herself. It was her baby, her masterpiece. She'd welded it together out of parts from the vast graveyard of ships that littered Jakku. Every single part in it was either scavenged or acquired in a trade with the Teedos. It had two stacked turbojet engines she'd pried out of an old cargo hauler, attached to amplifier intakes. She'd fitted on afterburners and repulsor-powered intake ducts from an old X-wing.

It was hard to pilot—top-heavy—and it

would roll if you didn't know what you were doing. That was fine with her; it just made it harder for anyone to steal. Besides, she'd rigged it with a fingerprint scanner and an intentionally loose hot wire. Whenever she was exploring a wreck, she attached that wire to the vehicle's hull. It was a great trick—electrified the whole thing. Anyone who touched the speeder would be zapped into the nearest sand dune.

And it was her only way to get around Jakku. Besides, she had no idea just what Unkar wanted hauled. It might not even be something she could manage, friends or no. Still—she'd never have survived so long on Jakku if she let a little risk scare her. Rey narrowed her eyes.

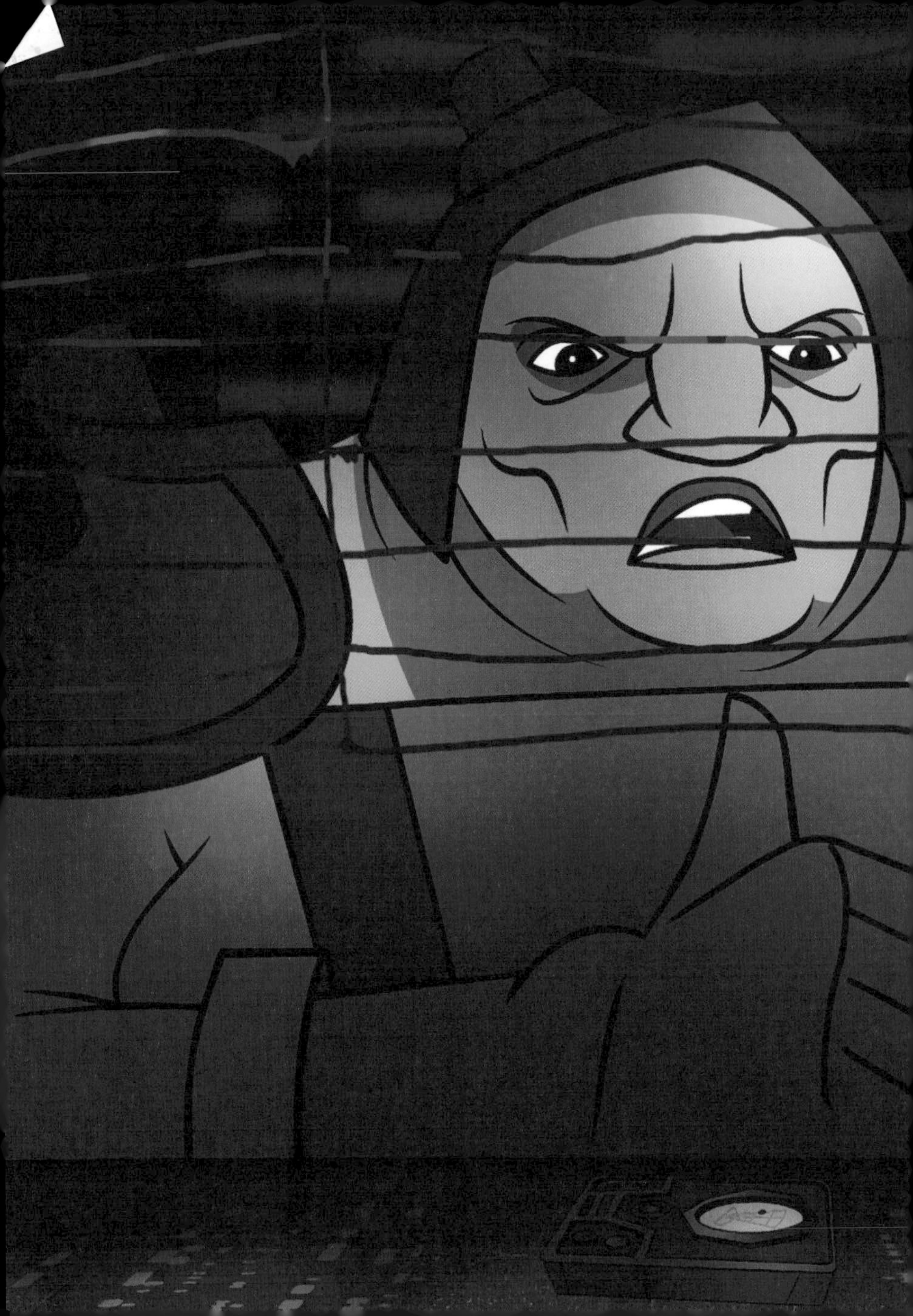

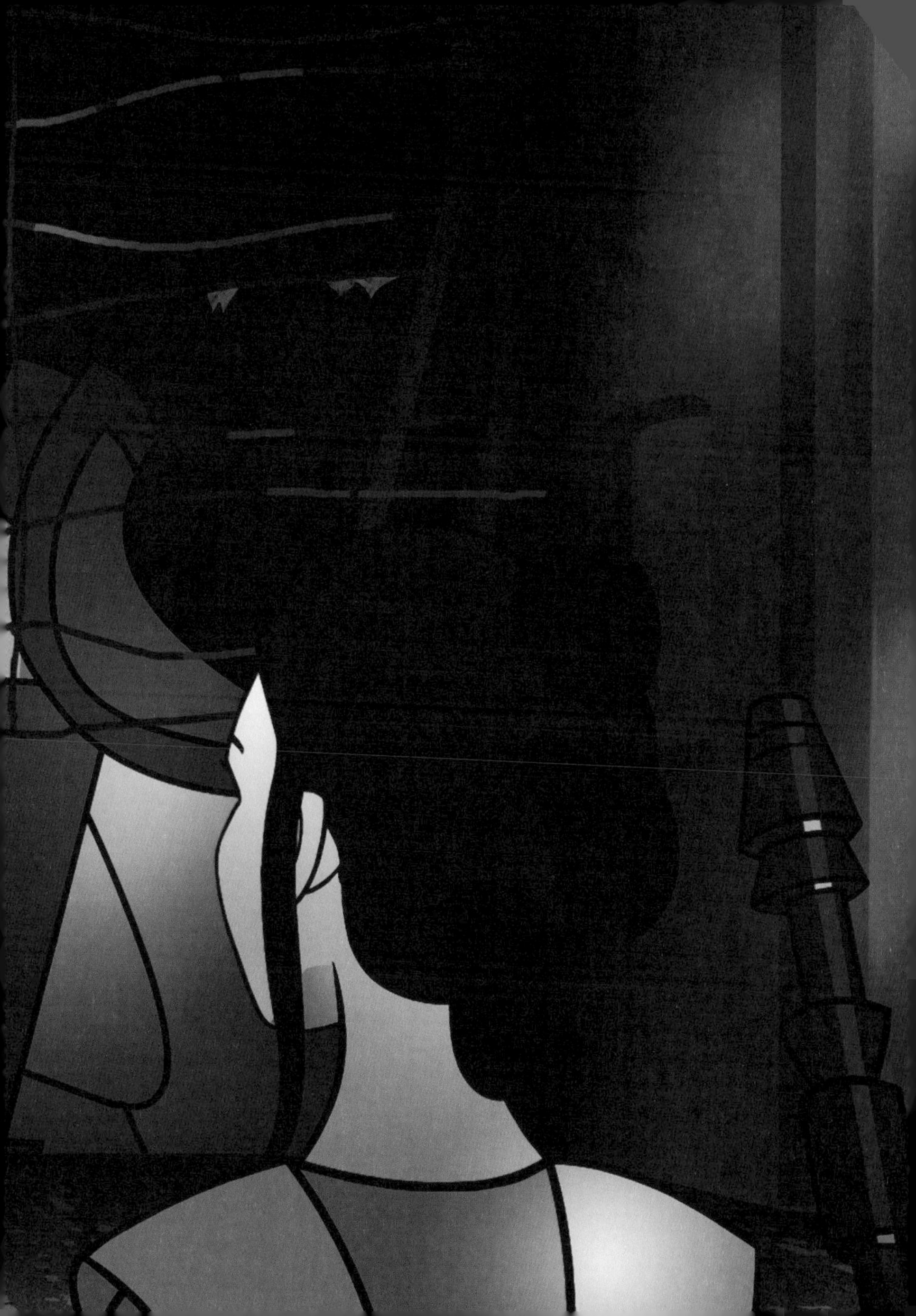

"If I'm risking my speeder, I want twenty portions when I deliver." She kept her tone careless. Unkar couldn't know how desperate she was.

He snorted.

"Ha! Here, and don't damage *my* speeder." He tossed Rey a locator. She caught it in one hand and leveled a cool stare at Unkar, then turned away, pulling down her goggles and wondering if she'd just ruined herself. She'd soon find out.

Half an hour later, Rey sped across the sand, passing the Sinking Fields on her left, heading deep into the western desert. The coordinates were leading her as far west as she'd ever been, into the rippling sandy nothingness. She squinted through her goggles.

She should be seeing it any minute. She scanned the horizon.

There! A large dark hulk loomed before her. She downshifted, the speeder's motor dropping to a low throb. She glided up to the thing and killed the motor. Her heart sank. It was a quadjumper—missing one engine—and huge. It lay mostly buried in the sand, deep drifts stacked against its sides. It was massive. And— Rey sighed—a gigantic happabore was lying against it.

She dismounted and eyed the beast. Happabores were massive and usually phlegmatic. They plodded through Jakku, giant snouts almost touching the ground, tiny eyes squinting so much it was a wonder they could see anything. They could crush you with their bite, and they could get pretty territorial around water, but generally they didn't move fast enough to get worked up about much. Their skin was so thick that it protected them from the heat, which was handy in a place like Jakku. She'd heard that they had reservoirs in their bodies that could hold liters of water. But this one must have been almost depleted. It looked like it had been there for a while: its armor-like gray hide was dry and dusted with sand. The wind had blown the sand up in piles around its short, stubby legs, too, half-burying them, just like the ship's hull.

"I can't move this ship with you here," Rey said. Her voice was small in the windy vastness.

The happabore opened one tiny bleary eye. It released a long groan, like a tire deflating, then closed its eye again.

Rey gritted her teeth.

"And Unkar knew you'd be here, too, didn't he? That's why he was paying so many portions." There was nothing to do but try to move the beast. She looked ruefully around. It wasn't as if there was anyone nearby to help her. Or anyone nearby at all.

"Okay, up you go!" Rey tugged at the happabore's neck. She might as well have been trying to move a boulder. She switched to shoving, bracing her hands on its hot prickly skin.

"Come on, come on!"

The happabore grunted and settled more firmly against the side of the ship. Rey poked it in the side with her staff. Nothing. She nudged it in the head. Nothing. She trudged around and jabbed it in the backside.

"Come on!" she yelled.

The happabore shifted forward and for an instant, Rey thought she'd won. Then the creature collapsed back on the sand, centimeters from where it had started.

"Argh!" Rey growled. Frustration boiled up in her and she ran on top of the happabore, right onto its huge ribcage, and jumped up and down.

"Move! Move! Move!" she shouted.

The beast raised its head and looked at her quizzically, then dropped it back down on the sand as if Rey were nothing more than a gnat buzzing around its ears. *Go ahead. You just jump around up there all day. Doesn't bother me a bit,* Rey could practically hear it thinking.

She heaved a great sigh and slid down the happabore's side, collapsing next to it on the hot sand. For a long moment, she just sat, head down, hands dangling between her updrawn knees. She was hot, she was sweaty, she was exhausted, and she was about to lose her speeder. So really, it couldn't get any worse. She might as well eat the quarter portion she'd saved from the previous night.

She shoved her goggles up on her head and unwound her dusty head wrap. Digging in her waist pouch, she pulled out the ration and

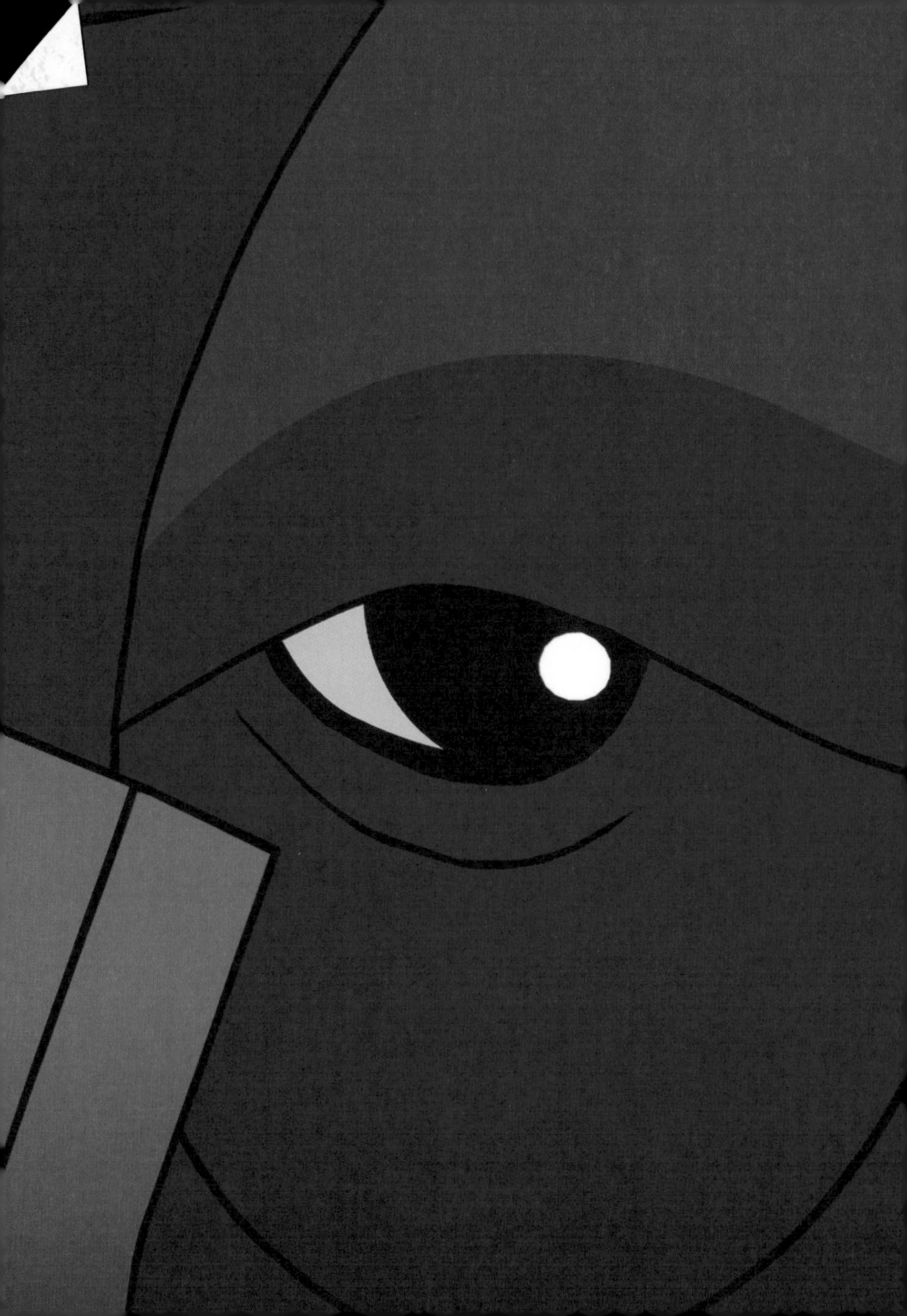

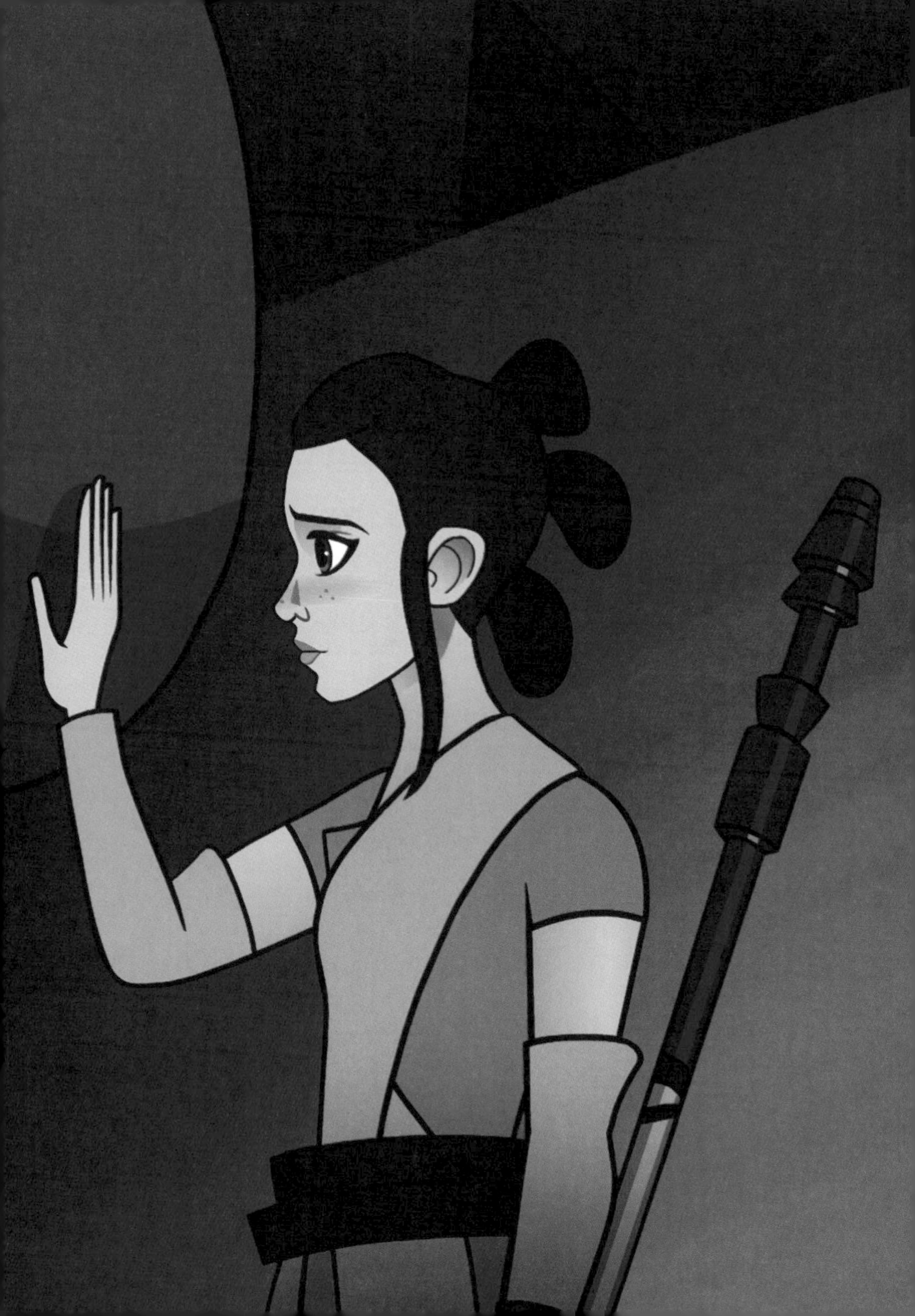

regarded it sadly, trying to push the thought of twenty portions out of her mind. She took a big bite and chewed—then her jaws froze. Some sort of strange sound was coming from the happabore, like a whistling—or a wheezing.

Rey stared at the animal. It was still lying on its side, immovable as a stone, its little eyes half-closed. She shoved the rest of the bread into her mouth and crawled over to it. The wheezing seemed to be coming from its snout—or muzzle, whatever it was called.

She bent over so she was closer to the happabore's snout. The wheezing *was* coming from in there. Rey bent closer. *Urgh.* Its breath was like rotten fish. Wrinkling her nose, Rey peered into the creature's nostril. There was something lodged in there. Rey sat up.

"That's it—you can't breathe!" That's why the happabore wouldn't move; it couldn't get enough air.

Suddenly, Rey realized what she had to do.

"Oh, no." She looked at the happabore and shook her head vigorously.

"No. No. Seriously?"

The creature opened one eye and looked at her again. Rey imagined it looked a tiny bit desperate. And *she* certainly was desperate.

"This wasn't what I had in mind!" she shouted into the empty air, shaking her fist.

She squeezed her eyes shut, then opened them again.

"Okay. Here we go."

She crouched down again on the sand in front of the happabore's head, then patted it on its wide slimy nose. Gritting her teeth, she slowly slid her hand into the cavernous nostril. Slippery. Moist. Rey cringed but kept reaching. How far *back* was the thing? She was practically up to her elbow already.

From her nostril-level vantage point, Rey saw the happabore's eye go wide.

"Sorry about this, fella," she muttered.

"Believe me, it's for the best."

The happabore whuffed and snorted. It inhaled sharply, as if it might sneeze.

"No, no, no, let's not do that!" she pleaded, still reaching.

The creature stirred and whuffed again. Rey's arm was jerked around inside the tunnel-like nostril.

"Let's not break my arm, please," she told it.

"I'm trying to help, here, in case you didn't notice."

She reached a little farther. Gah, she was up to her shoulder. If she couldn't get the thing out . . . Then the tips of her fingers brushed something hard, rough-edged, covered with a light layer of happabore snot.

Just a little farther . . . Rey reached in, her mouth hanging open with the effort. Her fingers could grasp the thing now.

"Got it!" She tugged, then tugged again. The object was wedged tight. No wonder the poor creature couldn't breathe.

Suddenly, a deep rumbling came from within the happabore. Rey barely had time to grasp the object before the happabore sneezed. An explosive heave of air pushed her backward, sending her flying through the air. She tumbled onto the sand and came to rest in a heap.

Rey sat up, covered in sand and mucus. She looked down at her own hand. Grasped tight in her fingers was the thing that had been jamming the beast's nose—a power converter about thirty centimeters long and twenty-five centimeters wide.

The happabore suddenly inhaled. Rey looked up. The creature's eyes were open all the way, and as Rey watched, it blew its breath out and shook its head vigorously. Rey didn't dare move. She kept her gaze fixed on the beast.

The happabore tucked its stubby legs underneath it and with a massive effort heaved its bulk from the ground. The stranded ship

shifted in the sand, one end rising from the
dune with the weight of the happabore gone.

"Yes!"

Rey thrust her fist in the air. The
happabore bellowed back as if it understood,
and Rey slapped its calloused shoulder.

"Well, you're welcome," Rey told it.
"Thanks for saying so."

Twenty sweaty minutes later, Rey had
secured the ship behind her speeder using a
complicated system of cords and knots. She
mounted the seat and gripped the handlebars.

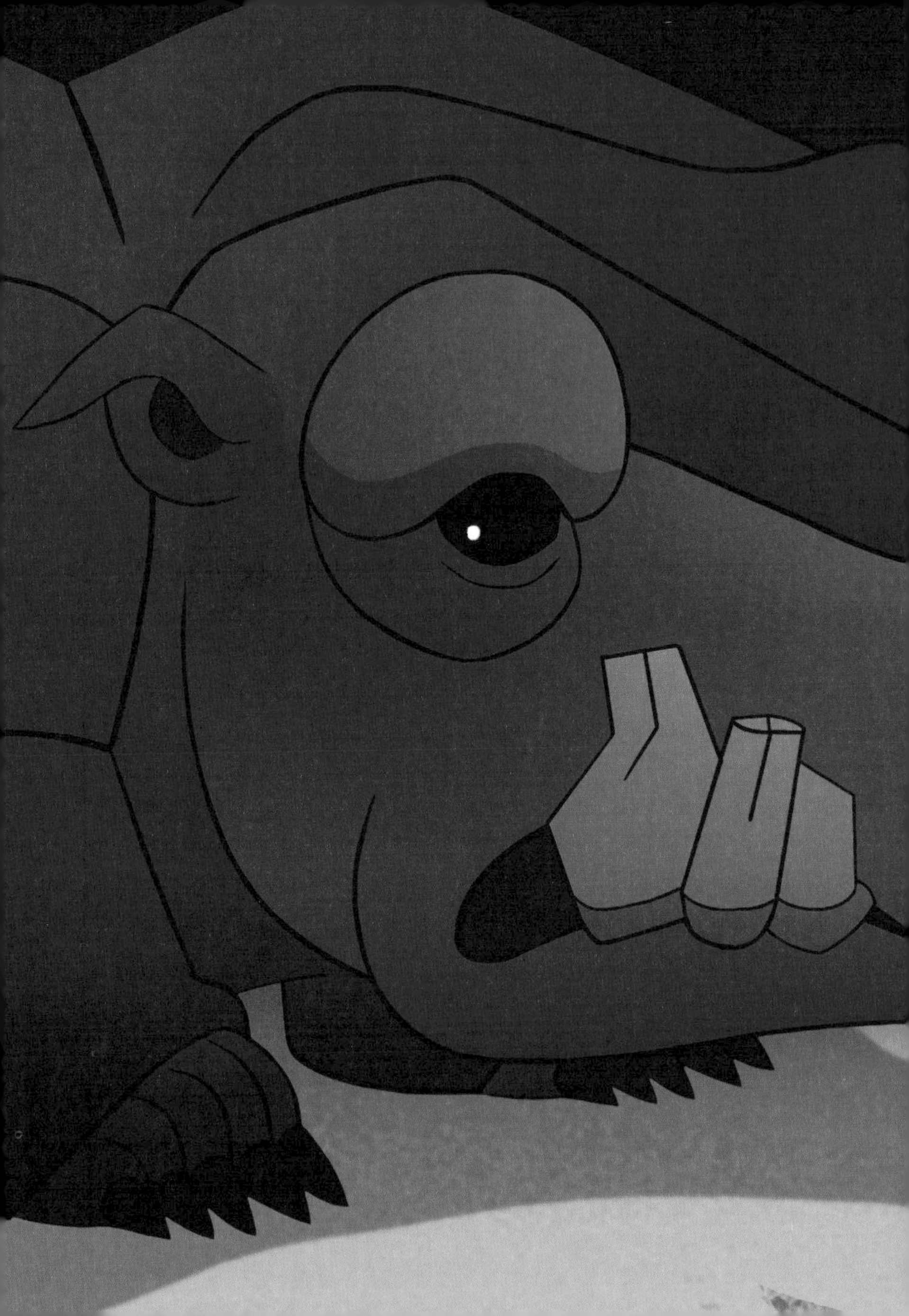

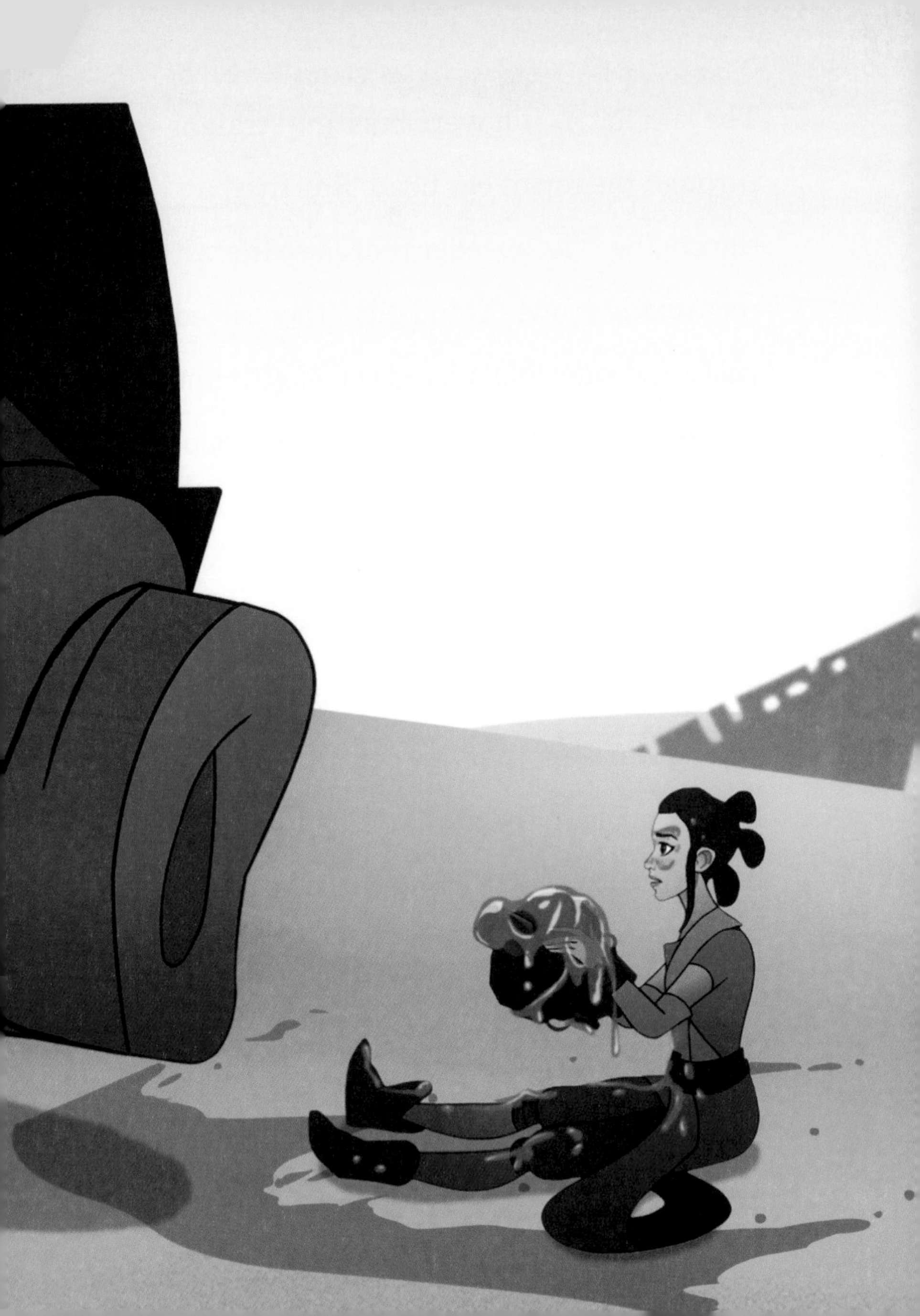

The sun felt as if it were burning straight through the top of her head. Rey fired up the engine. The speeder roared to life with a reassuring growl. "Good girl." Rey patted the rusty-red side. She revved the engine and the speeder surged forward—and then stopped.

Rey looked behind her. The quadjumper had moved only a short distance. She could see the drag marks in the sand. She clenched her teeth and fired the motor again. The ship slid forward another few centimeters, leaving her hovering in the air like a fool, tied to her bargain with Unkar along with the massive piece of junk.

"I don't believe this," Rey muttered to herself, and leaned forward over her handlebars. What was she going to do?

Suddenly, the speeder jolted forward, throwing her behind the seat. Rey bolted upright and pushed herself forward, twisting around to look. The happabore stood behind the ship, and—Rey could hardly believe her eyes—it was shoving the ship forward with its massive blunt head. As she watched, the happabore shoved the junk again, pushing it through the sand as if through water. The speeder, still in forward gear, jolted again, this time almost unseating her completely.

"Brilliant!" Rey yelled. She revved the engine.

"Let's go!" she called back to the happabore. Together they began moving the piece of junk slowly through the sand. Rey twisted around and beamed at the happabore, its skin cracked

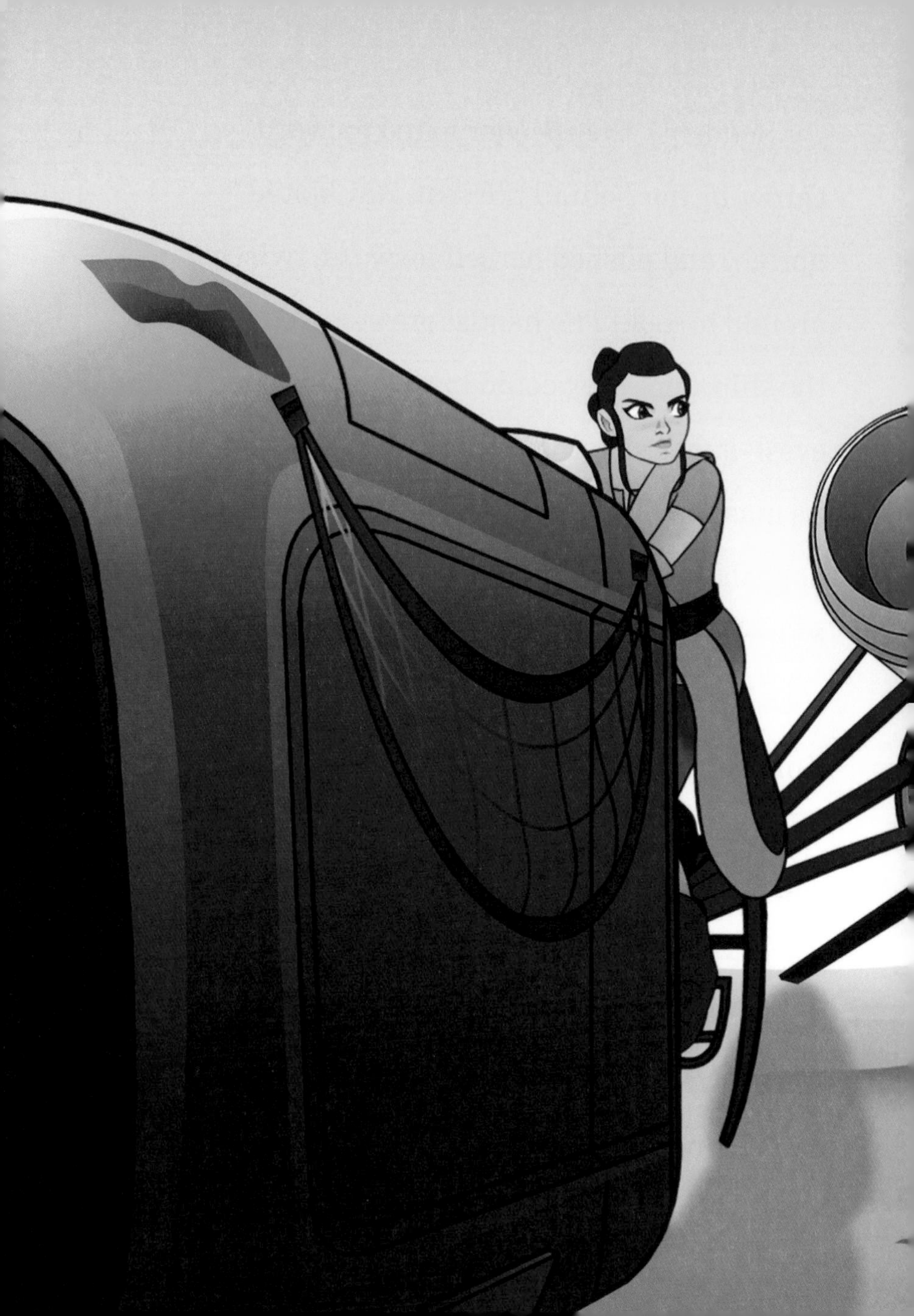

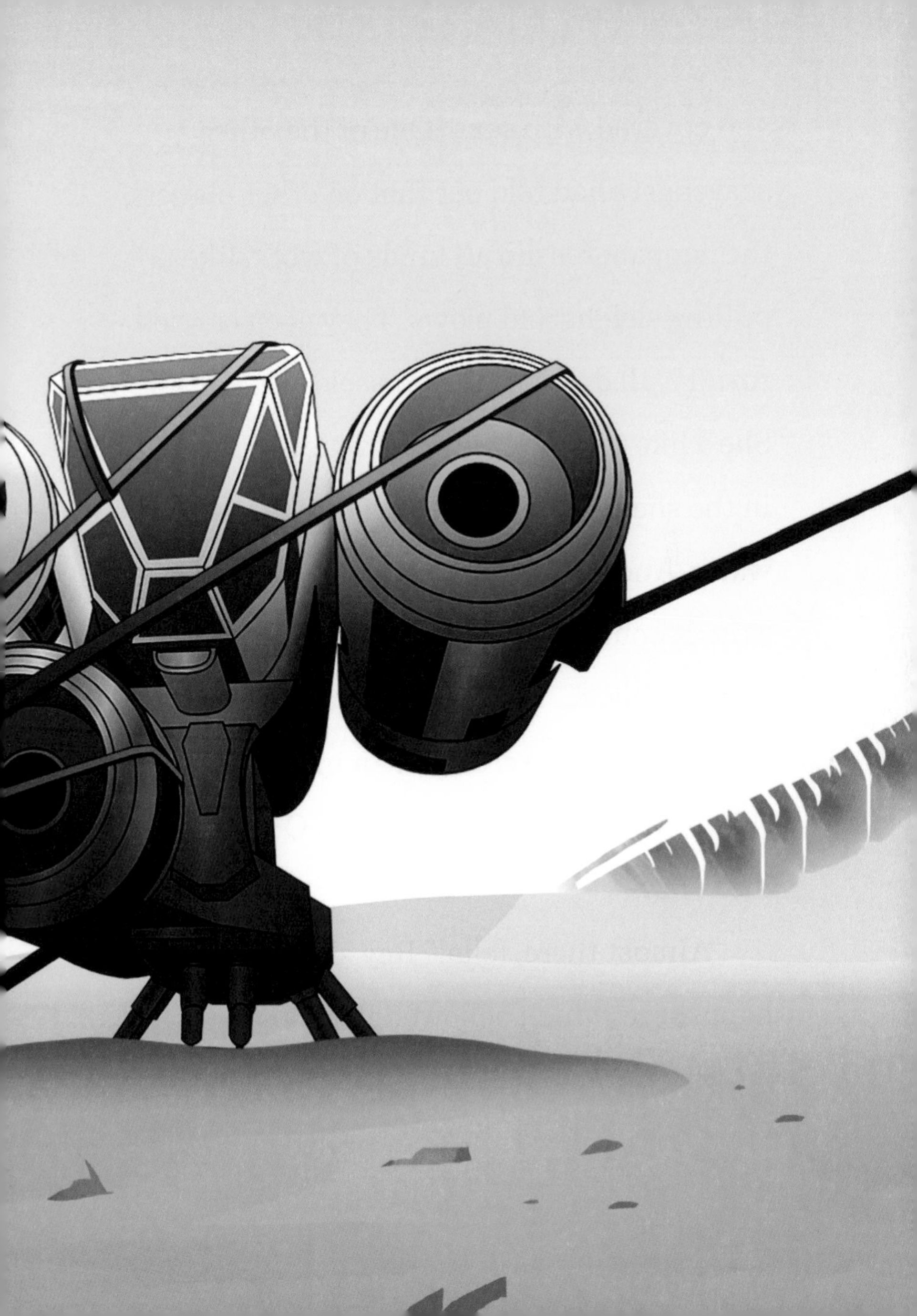

and covered with sand. One of the other scavengers had told her that on other planets, the happabores did all kinds of work, like pulling sleighs and plows. They even carried royalty, all dressed up in tassels and red silk. She'd like that for this one—a nice roomy pen in the shade, plenty of hay to eat, lots of cool water. And she'd find some salve for its broken skin. It could hang out in its pen and she'd visit it every day.

The sun was setting in an inferno of red flames when the stalls of Niima Outpost came into view.

"Almost there, fella!" Rey shouted to the happabore, which bellowed in return.

She gunned the engine and the happabore broke into a slow trot. They pulled up to the outskirts of the outpost just as Unkar was closing his shop shutters. Despite her hunger and exhaustion, Rey relished the look of utter shock on his wide flabby face.

"I don't believe it—how . . . ?" Unkar grunted in confusion.

Rey killed the motor and slid off the speeder. She threw her arm around the happabore's bristly neck.

"I made a friend, that's how." She paused and allowed a grin to spread across her face. "And now you owe me twenty portions."

Unkar stood frozen, his mouth hanging open. The happabore released a happy bellow as Rey gave it a grateful squeeze.

REY AND TEEDO

At least it's cool in here. Rey grabbed a cable and rappelled into the vast interior chasm of the Star Destroyer. The wreck had lain in the Jakku sands for as long as she could remember, but not many ventured as far into the Graveyard as she was willing to go. So the wreck wasn't as picked over as some of the

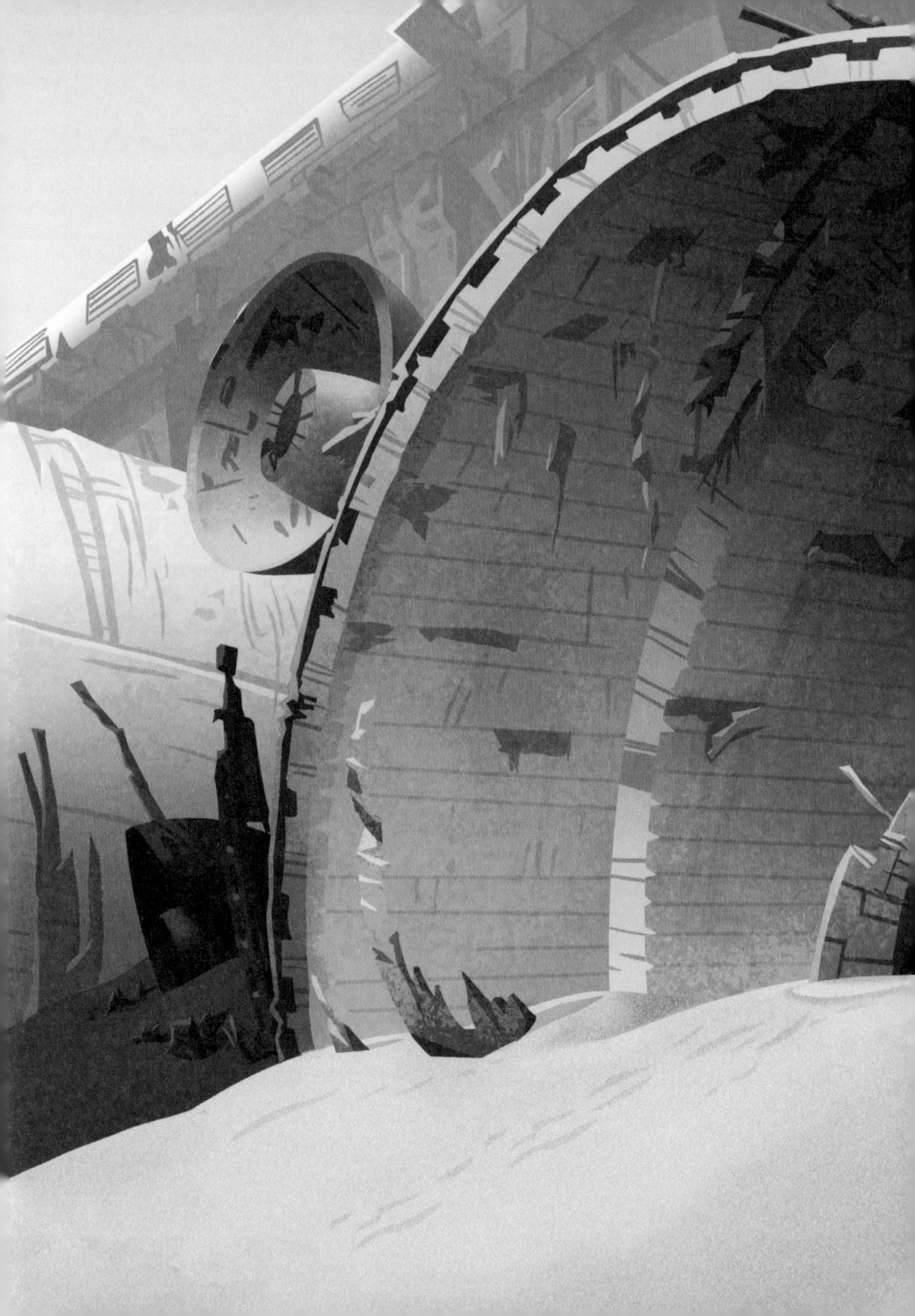

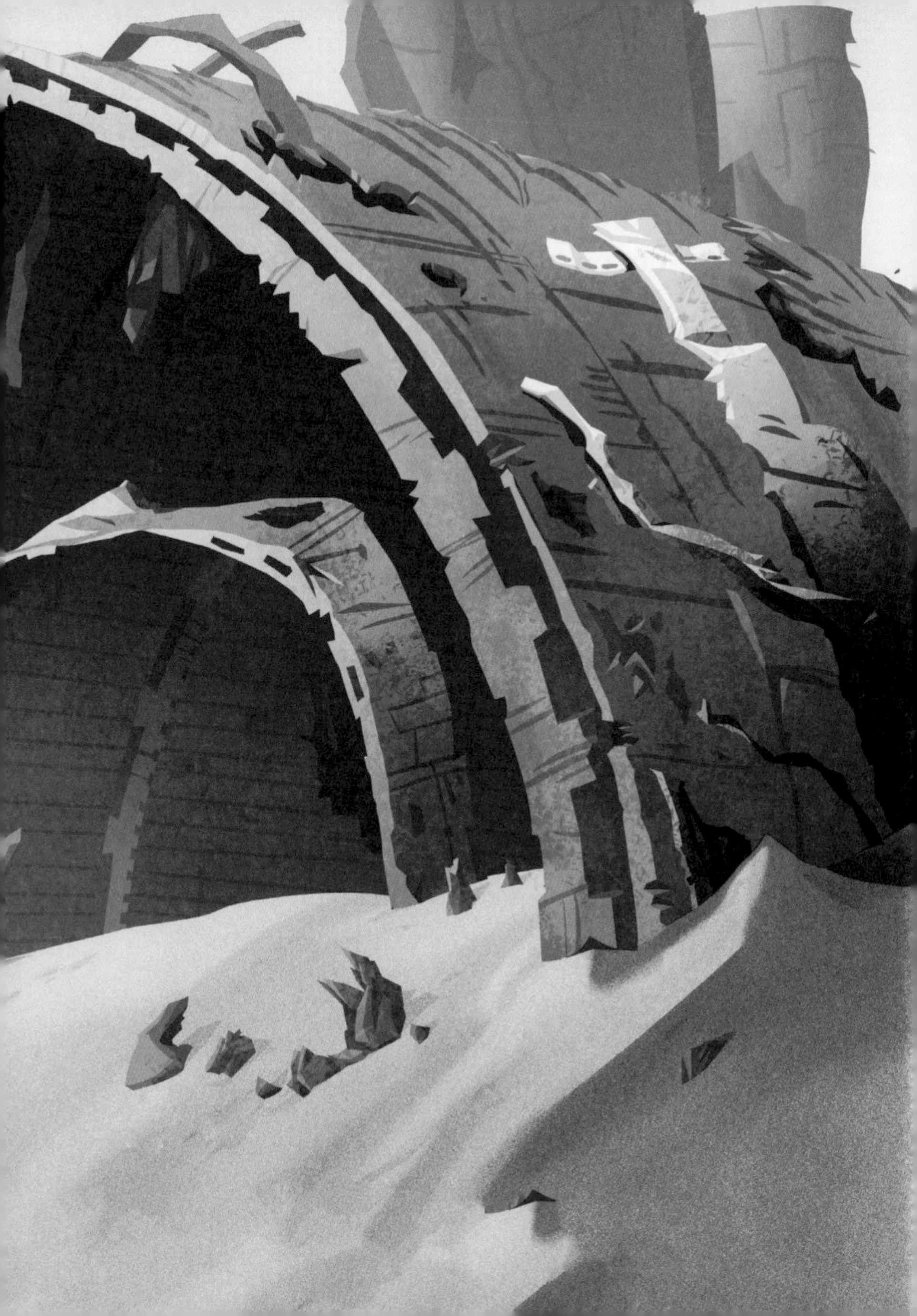

others. Rey swung through the dark gloom. The desert sun outside dotted the wreck with white-hot pinholes.

She hit the floor with a thud and released the cable. The engine room—that was what she needed to make her trip out there worthwhile. Rey trotted through the base of the Destroyer and climbed an interior wall, using the panel handles as her ladder.

Something shifted on the exterior of the ship and Rey froze. Was someone out there? Some of the more dangerous scavengers on Jakku sometimes went that far out. She didn't want to meet one.

"Hello?" she called.

Her voice echoed in the vast chamber. Nothing. Probably just a rodent of some kind.

Rey climbed up into what would have been the corridor leading to the engine room. Since it was flipped over and partly caved in, it was more like a tunnel now. As the ceiling narrowed, she crawled on her hands and knees through the darkness.

Reaching the engine room, Rey straightened up and eyed the giant turbines in the middle.

"Not there . . ." she muttered to herself. Unkar wasn't looking for those. Rey circled around and examined the hatch at the base of the turbine. If she could just get in there . . . She switched on her headlamp, aiming a blue-white beam at the latch. It looked damaged, probably from the crash. Rey pulled a wrench from her tool pouch and worked at the latch. Stuck. She spat on it, then pried at it again. It popped open with a rusty squeal.

"There." She stuck the wrench back in her pouch with satisfaction and poked her head and shoulders into the space. If she twisted around, she could see up into the giant column of the turbine. There they were. She had known she'd find some there. Rey reached up toward the red ignitor plugs. Unkar should pay at least two portions apiece for those. She pried all five loose and dropped them into her pouch.

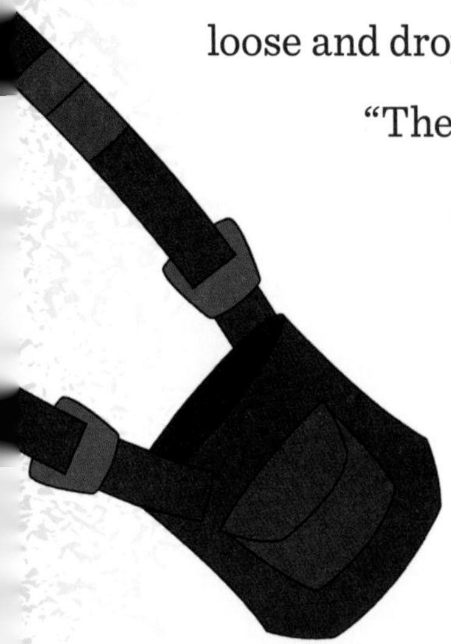

"There, these should work perfectly."

She started to wiggle out of the column when a flash of yellow caught her eye. Yellow!

She hadn't seen yellow

ignitor plugs on a Destroyer in a long time. Unkar would probably give five portions for one of those.

Moving carefully, Rey flipped open her pouch again and slid out the wrench. One thing she'd learned over the years was that she *was* her tools. Wrong tools—she couldn't expect to eat anytime soon. She'd worked up a pretty good tool pouch over the past several years: Pilex bit drivers with both Wessex and Blissex heads, a whole bag of quick-switch modulators. She'd started carrying Mon Calamari hex clamps and cruciform Verpine ratchets after she found herself in an X-wing fighter wreck a couple of years before. There had been a whole cache of batteries and she couldn't remove a single one because she didn't have the ratchets and clamps. She also had hydrospanners in all the eight standard configurations, with spare power cells; it had taken her some sweaty hours negotiating with Miggs McKane to trade for those. Microlenses came in handy for checking for tiny cracks. Most scavengers didn't bother with them, but Unkar would pay extra for pristine glass. And she always had a datapad with the schematics of every ship she'd ever found. That way she could orient herself instead of wandering lost around some ship, falling into a chasm, and breaking a wrist.

That was a great way to wind up dead on Jakku—not from the wrist but because then she couldn't climb out of the wreckage. Twenty-four hours at the bottom of a fifteen-meter hull and she'd be dead, her body drying in the sun and wind.

She wriggled farther into the turbine and worked the wrench around one of the plugs. Got it. She tugged. A tremendous moaning and creaking suddenly shuddered through the ship all around her. Rey stopped, the wrench still clamped around the ignitor plug. These ships looked everlasting, but Rey knew from experience they were held together with little more than decaying wire. A big wind could collapse a wreck like this one.

Rey wiped the sweat out of her eyes with one end of her head wrap, gritted her teeth, and tugged once more. She jumped as the ship shuddered again, and then she whipped around, trying to spot any metal paneling that might be coming loose. The plug must be attached to the main engine line, which was supporting the turbine, which was supporting the main hull. The plug was basically holding up the whole ship.

"Aaaand . . . I'll just leave this one alone," she whispered.

She backed away from the turbine, tucking the wrench back into her pouch. Suddenly, the engine room entrance darkened.

"Teedo!" Rey sucked in her breath and gripped her staff. Just what she needed. What was he doing so far out, anyway?

The little creature walked toward her, goggles shielding his eyes, blaster in hand. He pointed it directly at her.

"Give me the bag," he said in his harsh language. He pointed at her collecting sack.

Rey backed away, eyeing the blaster. Teedos didn't scare her, but no one knew much about them. No one she knew had

even seen one without its wrappings—just glimpses of scaly gray-green skin poking out, three-fingered hands, and feet with two toes in the front and one toe in the back. Under all those wrappings, they had a whole system of filters and tubes to recycle water. And they had scanners that could pick up on energy from the ships, so they knew where to scavenge. Rey generally didn't mess with them; their spears were ionized and they'd fight anything and anyone over scrap. The other weird thing about them was that all Teedos were named Teedo. And she knew this one well. She'd dealt with him before.

And he had a blaster. If she'd learned anything during her time on Jakku, it was not to argue with anyone holding a blaster in an enclosed space. She considered trying to knock it out of his hand with her staff.

"Teedo. You've been following me," she said.

He advanced on her and raised the blaster, gesturing toward her bag with it. His meaning was clear: *Hand it over.*

Rey squinted in frustration and gritted her teeth. Again! If only she could get a blaster of her own. Burning with impotent rage, she thrust the bag at Teedo.

"Fine. Take it." She spit the words at him.

Teedo opened the bag and examined the contents, clanking around the pieces inside.

"Very nice," he said in Teedospeak.

"Still . . ." He looked around and spotted the yellow ignitor plug.

"Yellow! Very rare." He examined it with interest, blaster still trained on Rey. She watched as he pried at it.

"You don't want to do that, trust me," she said.

He laughed.

"Shut up." He pulled out a wrench like hers and tried to dislodge the plug as she had.

"No, wait!" Rey lunged toward him, but he shoved her backward with one hand, yanking at the plug at the same time. She fell against the wall as he pulled the plug loose and shoved it in her bag.

A tremendous groan echoed through the ship and the walls began shaking. Bolts, panels, and cables rained down as the massive Destroyer started to collapse around them. "Now you've done it!" Rey shouted, covering her head with her arms. Teedo looked around wildly, clutching the collecting bag against his chest. Then a chunk of metal fell from the ceiling onto his head with a thud. Rey winced. Teedo hit the floor with all the grace of a bag of wet sand.

For a moment, Rey regarded him, lying unconscious in a heap on the floor.

"Well, that's just fantastic," she muttered. Then another shudder shook the ship. A huge door clattered down not five centimeters away. Rey pulled her goggles back down decisively and, leaning over, eased her collecting bag from under Teedo's body. She turned away. She had to make it to the opening before the hull collapsed.

Teedo stirred and moaned faintly, then lay still again. Rey stopped. She couldn't just leave him.

A series of cables snapped overhead one by one, like the too-taut strings of an instrument, and Rey winced as the frayed steel whipped near her face.

"Oh, for . . ." She strapped her bag across her chest and bent down, heaving Teedo over her shoulders. She staggered slightly under his weight. He smelled like unwashed shirts and sweat.

"You better appreciate this, you little . . ." she muttered.

She looked around, wincing as more panels and metal bits rained down around them. The deck of the ship groaned and buckled beneath her feet as she lurched, grabbing the wall for support under Teedo's weight.

Then she saw it—a faint white light gleaming far back in the depths of the ship. An opening! But it was so far back—how in the world was she going to get all the way over there with Teedo weighing her down like so much junk? She could barely walk two steps. Then the long shadow of a cable hanging into the depths of the ship caught her eye. In a flash, Rey knew what she was going to do.

A deep clang echoed from the depths of the ship. She didn't have much time. Rey eyed the distance between the edge of the platform and the rope. It was going to be close. She gritted her teeth. A tremendous chunk of turbine suddenly thudded down centimeters away, spraying them both with splinters of metal.

"I think we've outstayed our welcome here, don't you?" Rey muttered to the pile of rags that was Teedo.

She ran, staggering under Teedo's weight, and leapt with all her might into the chasm, grabbing for the cable at the same time. For one heart-stopping instant, she felt the void beneath her. Then the cable thumped into her hand, beautifully solid, and she and Teedo zipped down the cable, onto the next level beneath them. They landed in a heap, but Rey got them up and moving again quickly.

"Hunnh!" Teedo suddenly jerked away, thrashing around and flailing his arms.

"Hold still!" Rey shouted, lurching.

"Don't you know when someone's trying to help you?" she snapped.

The opening loomed ahead, and the bright sunlight dazzled her eyes. Rey jumped onto a large piece of scrap metal and rode it like a sled through the opening, out into the vast yellow desert, the huge ship crumbling behind them like the skeleton of an ancient beast.

They skidded to a halt in the sand, both Teedo and her bag going flying. Teedo crashed down nearby, yelling in panic and anger.

"Oooh." Rey pushed herself up. Her brain felt scrambled. She rubbed her fists into her eyes. She was covered in grease and tiny glittering bits of metal. One whole side of her body was caked with sand. But she was alive— there was that.

Suddenly, out of the corner of her eye, she saw a gray-green hand creeping toward her collecting bag.

"Hey! Give me that!" Rey shouted, lunging for the bag.

Teedo made a quick grab and got it. Rey snatched the other end.

"That's mine, Teedo!" She pulled with all

her might, but Teedo wrenched it out of her grasp.

He climbed to his feet and darted a few meters away, clasping the bag to his chest.

Rey climbed to her feet. She clenched her jaw and stared right at Teedo.

"You know, you're heavier than you look."

"What do you mean?" Teedo growled. He looked down at his paunchy belly.

"I mean, hand it over." Rey held her hand out. She kept him fixed in her stare, hoping he would give in. She didn't have any way of forcing him, except appealing to his conscience.

Teedo hesitated, gripping the neck of the bag.

"Come on." Rey waved her hand at him.

Did Teedo even *have* a conscience? She'd never really thought about it.

Grumbling unhappily, Teedo slowly extended the bag toward her. Rey took it and relief washed over her.

Then she saw something red half-concealed in his hand. An ignitor plug! He must have snuck it out of the bag. Rey leveled a steady look at Teedo.

"I did just save your life," she said.

For a long moment, he clutched the ignitor plug. Rey held her breath. Then he tossed the plug to her. Rey plucked it easily out of the air and ran for her speeder. She didn't need to wait around for Teedo to change his mind.

She slipped the bag into its sling on the side

of the speeder, threw her leg over the seat, and fired up the accelerator. Gunning the engine, she lowered her goggles and leaned low over the handlebars. As she zoomed away, she looked back at Teedo, standing forlorn in the middle of the sand.

"And you're welcome!" she shouted over her shoulder.

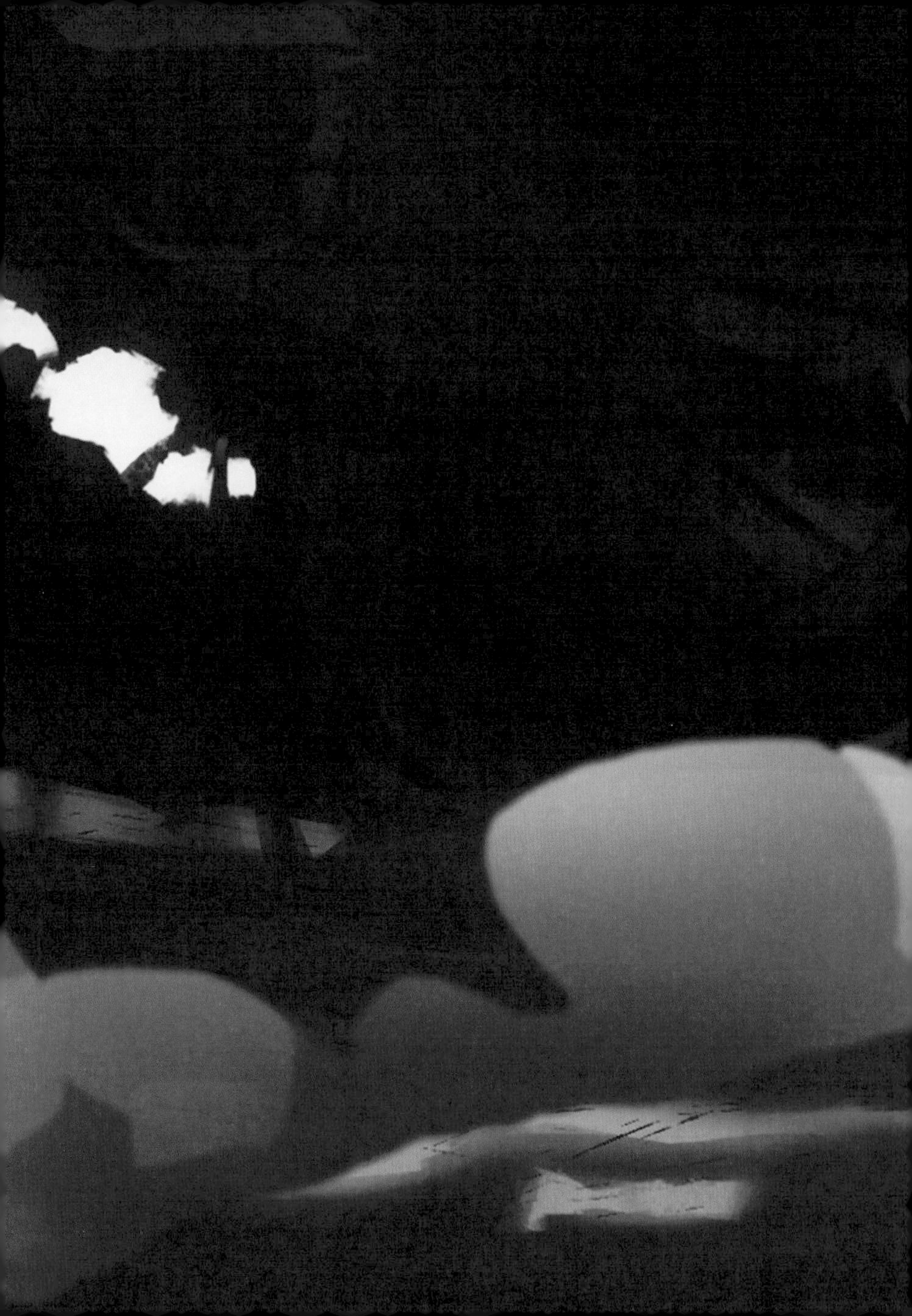

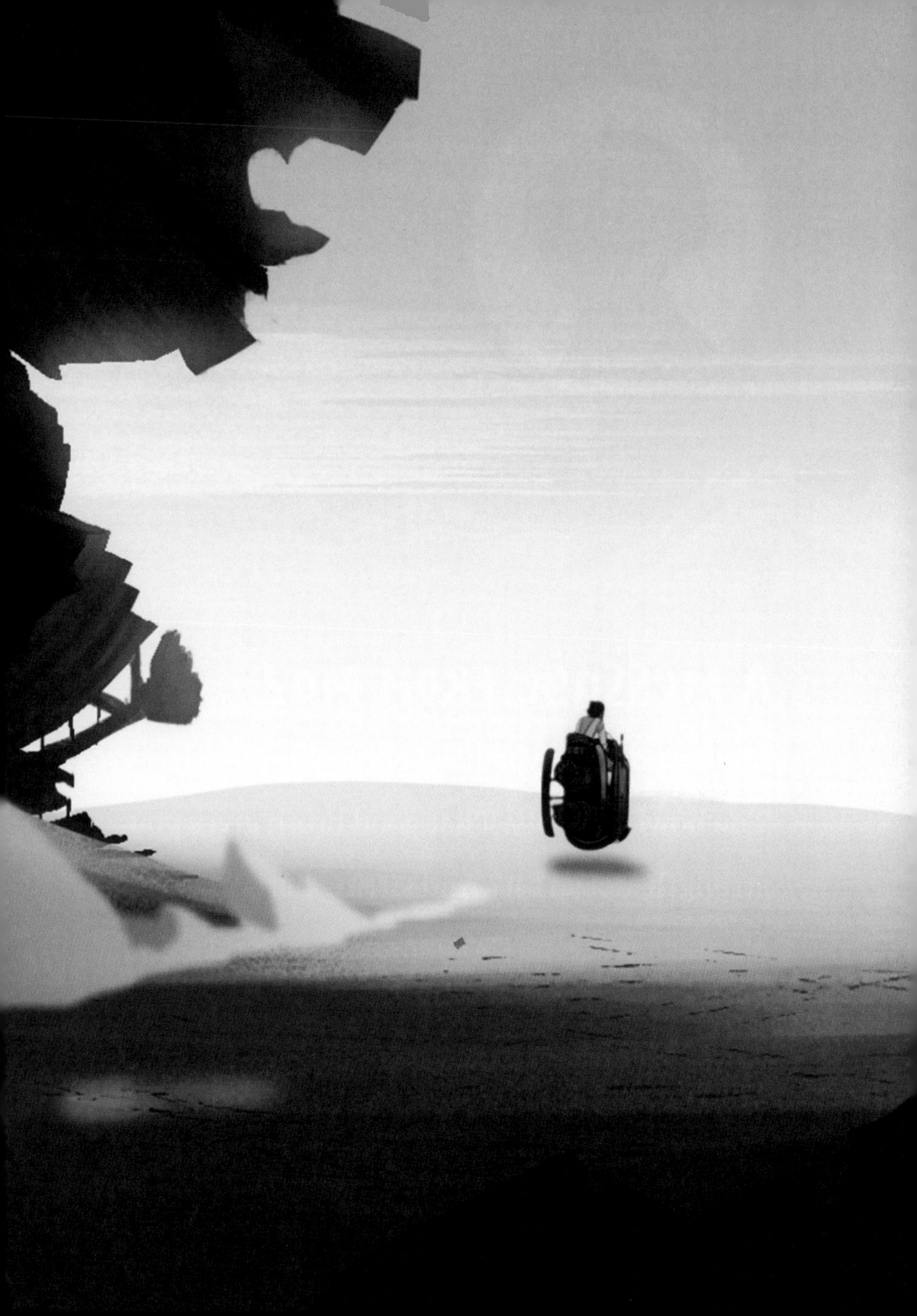

A MESSAGE FROM MAZ

My friend, I see you have eaten your broth.
The bowl is empty. That good broth gives you
strength, doesn't it? And sitting here, with this
blanket over your shoulders. Warm and soft, is
it not? It was given to me by a friend. Now I've
offered it to you, my tired fighter. I am glad you
have been able to rest. I am glad I have been

able to care for you. I don't think many people have done that in your life. No? As I thought. You have always fought, kept yourself strong like the stag antler.

And you must keep fighting. I think you know that. Not always with your muscles, though. Your spirit must keep fighting. Your

love and compassion must keep fighting. Never allow the forces of darkness to overpower your light. I am glad I could give you tea, broth, a blanket. It is not good to be hard all the time. Do you feel stronger? You do? Good. Now you can return to the battle—stronger than before.

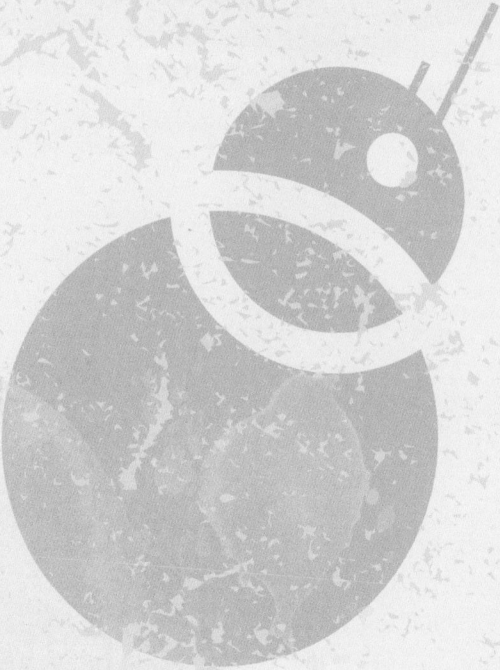

ABOUT THE AUTHOR

EMMA CARLSON BERNE has written many books for children and young adults, including historical fiction, sports fiction, romances, and mysteries. She writes and runs after her three little boys in Cincinnati, Ohio.

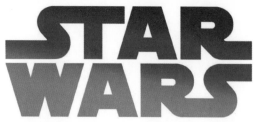

STAR WARS
FORCES OF DESTINY™

COLLECT THEM ALL!

Set of 4 Hardcover Books ISBN:
978-1-5321-4324-3

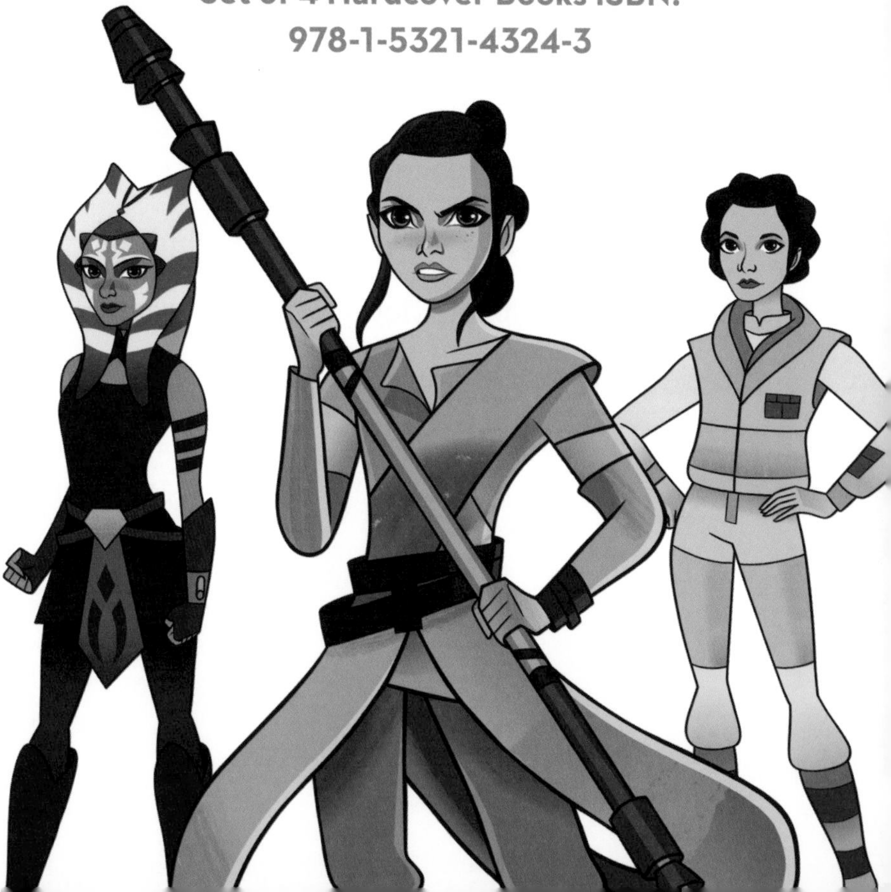

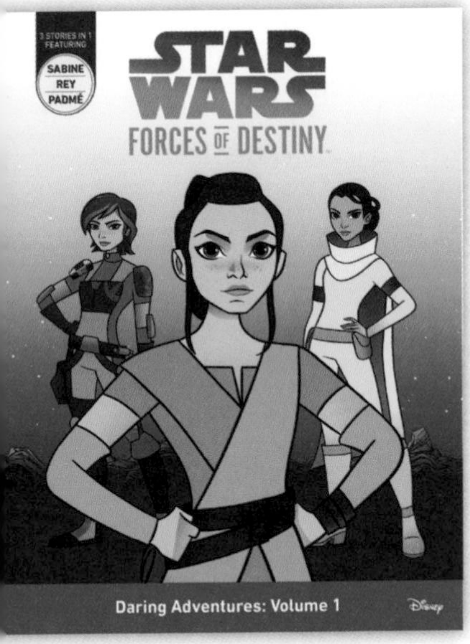
3 STORIES IN 1 FEATURING
SABINE
REY
PADMÉ
STAR WARS
FORCES OF DESTINY
Daring Adventures: Volume 1

Hardcover Book ISBN
978-1-5321-4325-0

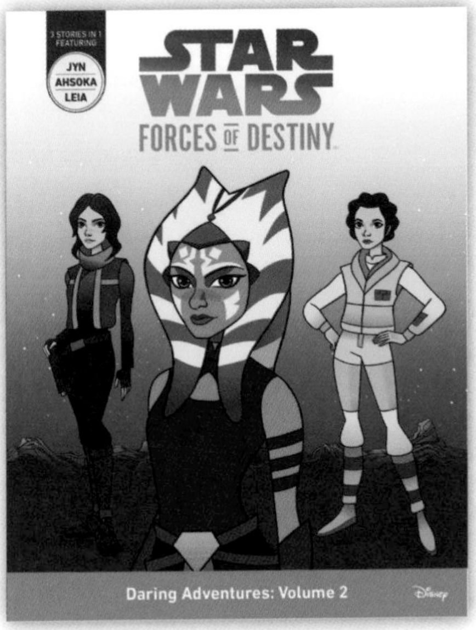
3 STORIES IN 1 FEATURING
JYN
AHSOKA
LEIA
STAR WARS
FORCES OF DESTINY
Daring Adventures: Volume 2

Hardcover Book ISBN
978-1-5321-4326-7

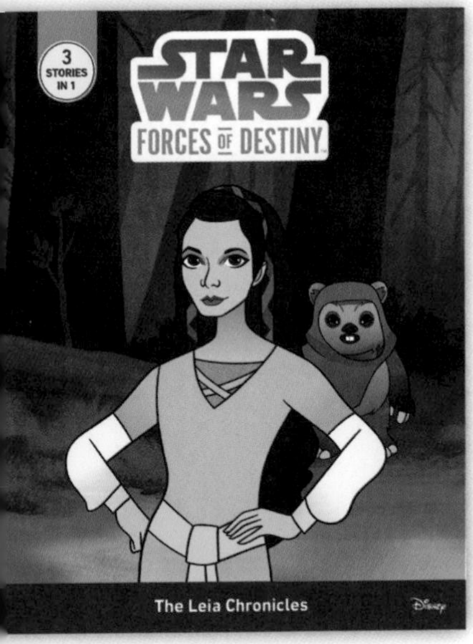
3 STORIES IN 1
STAR WARS
FORCES OF DESTINY
The Leia Chronicles

Hardcover Book ISBN
978-1-5321-4327-4

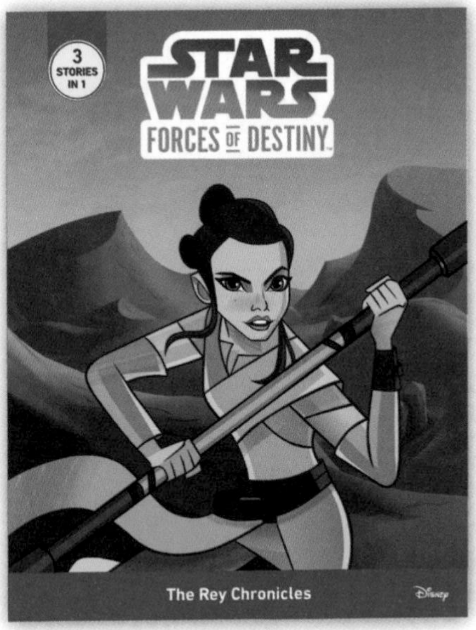
3 STORIES IN 1
STAR WARS
FORCES OF DESTINY
The Rey Chronicles

Hardcover Book ISBN
978-1-5321-4328-1